THE
VILLA

BEN ROLPHE

First Edition September 2012

Carpenter's Son Publishing
307 Verde Meadow Drive
Franklin, Tennessee 37067
Phone: (615) 472-1128
Larry@ChristianBookServices.com

ISBN: 978-0-9849772-1-5

Praises for THE VILLA

If you like Christian fiction series books, The Villa is a great book to check out. Even if you haven't read the first two books in the series, you can easily get into this novel. The author has a wonderful way of creating word pictures that can help you imagine the characters as if they were your own friends. – Brooke Golliher

The Villa is a very touching uplifting story of how even the impossible can be reality with the divine intervention of God. I loved seeing how a man takes a life filled with tragedy and with God's help carries on with a positive outlook. If you are going through hard times and need a glimmer of hope and happiness, this is a perfect book. – Amy Upton

Here is The Villa, the third book in Ben Rolphe's trilogy. The Branson family's struggles against all that is evil in the world we live today are nothing short of inspiring. They provide a constant reminder that in this day where nothing spiritual seems to matter to most how to be a family man in trying times. Being a devoutly spiritual man and Oregon resident, I couldn't wait for the final installment of this trilogy. With the amount of spiritual readings available for me to read, I rarely tackle fiction, but the author in each chapter reminds me why I should read more Christian fiction. – Brendan Bryne

Although most books in the spiritual market could not typically be described as "action-packed," The Villa by Ben Rolphe is not your ordinary spiritual novel. Rolphe proves that he is a master of fiction, incorporating elements of various genres, keeping his readers on the edge of their seats as each new plot twist unfolds. Fans of the first two books in the series will doubtlessly love this third installment, as will readers who are being introduced to Dan Branson and family for the very first time. – Brittany Walters

Praises for THE VILLA

The third book in a series about the Branson family, The Villa, by Ben Rolphe is a book about the power of God and just how important spirituality is. Following the lives of Dan Branson and his special family, Rolphe takes us on a journey into the hearts and souls of some dedicated followers of God. Threatened by the dangers of the world, the Branson family and friends must keep their faith strong as they encounter life's uncertainties. Watched over by God and His angel, Angelo, the family's faith is continually tested both at home on the Triple Peaks Ranch, and abroad in Central America. A heartwarming and easy read, The Villa is a great work of spiritual fiction that will strengthen the faith in all of us.   -Katie Shumacher

The Villa is the third installment by Ben Rolphe that follows the lives of a Gulf War veteran, Dan Branson, and his wife, Jessie, along with their two children, Mattie and Dan, Jr. The Oregon cattle rancher is once again pitted in his never-ending battle between evil and the Holy Spirit. Whether you are a believer or not, The Villa is a fantastic read.
                                                                    - Jeff Bearden

The Villa, the third fictional book in the series of Oregon's Branson Family members, is very good uplifting and enlightening and would appeal to anyone interested in Spirituality. Through continuation of the Branson Family's many challenges, especially Dan Branson's transition from Gulf War veteran to Oregon cattle rancher, the story touches on the perpetual struggle between good and evil, in short morality. The rustic Oregon setting adds to the story and almost reflects Dan Branson's somewhat tough and hard physique. Besides those looking for spiritual literature, The Villa would appeal to readers interested in the West Coast and the dynamics within a family.   - Sophia Solivio

Also by Ben Rolphe

- DAN BRANSON SERIES -

THE LIGHT

CHALLENGED

THE VILLA

Autobiography

APPOINTMENT WITH DESTINY

AFAB (ANYTHING FOR A BUCK)

*This book is for
those friends and family
who supported and encouraged me
to write spiritually oriented novels.*

*Very little is needed
to make a happy life. It is all
within each of us, in our imagination
and our creativity. Most important,
it is in our way of thinking.*

ACKNOWLEDGEMENT

I am compelled to concede that constant prayer and the guidance of God's Holy Spirit assisted me in writing this novel. I pray that words and the power of this story may touch the hearts of those seeking God's Peace.

Furthermore, this book would never have been completed without the support of my loving wife, Anna, who spent endless hours supporting me to the completion of this my third novel.

Additionally, I acknowledge my literary consultant, Larry Carpenter, my publicist, Kirsten Kamm, my editor, Lorraine Bossé-Smith and my proofer Bob Irvin. Their combined experience, wisdom and knowledge provided valuable direction.

PROLOGUE

Previously, Dan Branson had been hired as the head wrangler for the Triple Peaks Ranch, located near Sisters, Oregon. Six years later, through a multitude of different circumstances, he became the owner of the spread.

A native of Montana, he was born and raised just north of the area between Bozeman and Livingston on a small farm/ranch still owned by his parents. Their property consisted of a quarter section (160 acres) of land, half open pasture and half native timber.

He spent the majority of his leisure time alone, concentrating on his studies, ultimately graduating number two in his class. Following graduation, he was granted a full scholarship to Montana State.

Dan took advantage of the scholarship and enrolled at the University located in Bozeman just 25 miles from his home, choosing to major in animal husbandry and forestry.

During his second year at the University, he was encouraged by a good friend to sign up for the Air Force ROTC Program. Dan soon realized that he was fascinated with aeronautics and totally enamored with the idea of becoming a pilot.

He graduated with honors from Montana State at age twenty-two, receiving two degrees: one in animal husbandry and the other in aeronautics. He joined the Air Force a month after graduation and spent the next year in pilot training at Sheppard Air Force Base located at Wichita Falls, Texas. Early in his year of pilot training, Dan met Abby Trenton, a second

1

lieutenant registered nurse. The two had met at a USO dance being held on the air base just prior to the Thanksgiving holiday. Abby was a stunningly beautiful woman. She was five-foot-seven and was clearly obsessed with maintaining her physical condition. She worked out and ran cross-country on a daily basis. She had short-cropped, naturally blond hair and wore very little makeup. She radiated a wholesome appearance as well as a striking beauty that caused people to stop and admire her.

They quickly were falling deeply in love. The two were never far apart and, thus, had become inseparable. Following two months of passionate romance, they were married by an Air Force Chaplain.

The couple had been married for nearly five months when Dan graduated from pilot training. Following his graduation, Dan was ordered to report to a KC135 tanker squadron based in Turkey. He would be making daily flights refueling UN aircraft involved in the prevailing Mideast war. Abby remained in Wichita Falls, continuing to work at the base hospital. Dan had been assigned to duty in Turkey for only a month when he was called home to be with his wife.

His bride of only five months had been involved in a tragic, traffic accident. A large cement truck lost its brakes and careened through an intersection, broadsiding her car. Abby, four months pregnant, died an hour after Dan's arrival as he held her hand in the intensive care unit of the base hospital.

Dan returned to his squadron located in Turkey. Following a grueling mission in extremely unstable air, Dan's aircraft was diverted to Baghdad where he was also advised that he would not be flying until late the following day.

He made the decision to visit a college friend located at a base 70 kilometers from Baghdad. While on his way to meet his buddy, his Humvee was struck by a rocket-propelled grenade. Although five people were in the Humvee, Dan was the one who survived the attack.

The head and back injuries Dan received as a result of the attack ended his piloting career with the Air Force. Following several months of intensive medical treatment, physical therapy, and counseling at an Air Force hospital located in Germany, he was pronounced completely healed, but not qualified for flying.

As a result of the recent tragic loss of his wife, as well as his own injuries, his superiors presented him with two options. He could either continue in the Air Force performing ground-based duties or, if he desired, he could resign his commission and go back to civilian life. Dan quickly accepted the option to resign from the Air Force. Dan's statement was that his "dream was to fly airplanes, not sit behind a desk."

After having spent nearly six years as general manager and head wrangler for the ranch, a life-changing incident impacted his life. He was walking to his cabin from the ranch's corral when a bright light, flashing between two snow-capped peaks high in the mountains, drew his attention. He couldn't get the flashing light out of his mind and decided to investigate the source.

A woman, who Dan assumed to be an extraterrestrial, stated that she had sent the light signals directly to Dan, expecting him to search out the source.

The woman, named Angie, encouraged Dan to describe his beliefs and philosophy pertaining to the entire world and its population. Dan expounded for hours, describing what he believed. He proclaimed that the world's population was doomed to self-destruction as a result of greed and immorality.

Dan, believing the woman to be an extraterrestrial, was cautious and suspicious of her presence. She claimed she was on a mission to share long-forgotten laws of physics to the leaders of the world. She adamantly stated that adverse forces wanted to keep her from fulfilling her mission. She challenged him to join her. Following very little deliberation, he agreed.

After experiencing several close calls and numerous challenges, he discovered that the woman he thought to be an extraterrestrial had transformed into one of God's Angels. She—who actually turned out to be a he—stated that his true name was Angelo. He had taken on the body and appearance of an actual woman living in southern Oregon. He stated that he, along with Michael, the Archangel, had been sent to seek Dan's assistance in accomplishing their goal.

Once the mission was completed and Dan had returned home, he was startled when a woman appearing to be the identical twin of Angie came to him to seek his help in training her young daughter, Mattie, to ride a horse.

This woman, calling herself Jessie, lived in southern Oregon. She presented Dan with an unopened letter, addressed to him, that she had received from a gentleman who had identified himself as Angelo. Dan knew instantly that this was the same Angelo, God's

4

Angel, whom he had met in the mountains. The woman explained that she didn't know the man; however, he had appeared to be very sincere and advised her to present the letter to Dan.

When Dan read the letter, he discovered that Jessie woman was none other than the former wife of the Marine lieutenant who had been killed by the rocket-propelled grenade that had struck Dan's Humvee in Iraq. Dan was not surprised that the letter had indeed been written by God's angel, Angelo.

Within a short time, Dan and Jessie were convinced that they were destined to be together. A few months later, they were married. Dan withdrew the money he had received from the insurance companies following his wife's death. He took the money he had deposited in the bank in Texas and purchased the Triple Peaks Ranch. Almost a year to the day following their wedding, Jessie gave birth to their son Danny. The time that had passed had been good to the Branson family and the Triple Peaks Ranch had prospered.

Mattie, now nearing the age of nineteen, has just completed her first year of studies at Multnomah University in Portland, Oregon.

Our story picks up here...

1

Dan and Jessie Branson stood midday among the crowd of cheering college students lining the large, lawn-covered field in the center of Portland, Oregon's Multnomah University campus.

They watched their daughter, Mattie, accompanied by five other students, being pushed in a small Volkswagen sedan across the giant field located in the center of the campus and into position at the starting line.

A total of four cars had lined up on the far end of the field before the flag had dropped. Obviously, this was to be a race to the finish line at the opposite end of the field.

All four cars had large numbers attached to the back and were maneuvered by three young men and three young women. The object was to arrive at the opposite end of the field ahead of the other three cars. Engines were not allowed as five would push while one girl would navigate and steer the car around the numerous obstacles that had been placed in each roped-off lane.

The yelling and screaming was deafening as the cars moved past Dan and Jessie on their way to the finish line. Jessie had covered her ears and was leaning into Dan to avoid being pushed to the ground by the students who were jumping as high as they could to observe the action happening in front of them.

Suddenly, Jessie jumped up and yelled, "That's Mattie's car out in front!"

Dan and Jessie watched as the little Volkswagen passed them and then suddenly slowed down as one of the girls pushing, fell. One of the boys on her team stopped pushing to run back and help the fallen girl to her feet. This was just enough time for Mattie's car to move from first to last position.

Finally, the cheering subsided, and the students stood motionless, waiting for the judges to hold up a large placard displaying the winning team's number. Mattie had been chosen by her teammates to steer car number three; the number displayed on the placard was number two. Loud cheers erupted from the supporters of the winning team accompanied by subdued moans directed at the teams of the other three cars.

The 'Volkswagen-Push-Race' is said to be a traditional, annual event that takes place near the end of each school year. No one could remember who had won the previous year as all had been quickly forgotten. A total of four races occurred before the winners of each of the races lined up for the final push to the finish line.

Amazingly, Mattie had found her parents in the milling crowd and now stood between Dan and Jessie. Mattie began to yell as loud as all of the other students rooting her friends in car number one to the finish line. Again, both cheers and moans were heard as the number four car crossed the finish line at least a car length ahead of the rest.

When the crowd began to disperse, Mattie took both of her parents by the hand and began to lead them across the field to a building she referred to as the SUB, more commonly known as the Student Union Building.

"Come on, you two, I want you to meet some friends of mine. They're waiting for us."

"Slow down, Mattie; you're going to drive your mom and me right into the ground. We're old folks now and aren't supposed to be able to keep up with you teenagers. Stop running and just walk with us."

"Hey, Dad, I'm not going to be a teenager much longer. I'm going to be twenty in a few months, remember?"

As they entered the building, at least a hundred students were all talking at the same time. They were all reliving the race event that had just concluded a few minutes earlier. The winners were congratulated, while the losers were telling everyone how circumstances had prohibited them from being the winning team. Actually, everyone was enjoying the moment.

Mattie led her parents to a small corner where two overstuffed couches faced each other. Two girls were sitting on one of the couches. Both of the seated girls were staring at Mattie with looks of anticipation on their faces.

Mattie turned to face her parents and proceeded to introduce both of the girls.

"Mom and Dad, these are my two best friends. This is Alicia Clark," she said as she pointed at one of the girls, "and this is Bethany Thomas," she said, pointing to the other girl sitting on the couch with Alicia.

Mattie stood between the two couches and pointed at the empty couch motioning for her parents to be seated, then took her seat between her two friends.

Natural blondes, the three girls wore their hair cut short. All were about the same height at five foot six. They radiated a youthful, wholesome appearance.

Appearing to be in top physical condition, they dressed alike, wearing jeans and sweat shirts with the school logo emblazoned across the front and back.

Mattie had mentioned that they were also running partners, committed to running three miles each day.

"We have something we need to tell you and also, we are asking for your blessing."

Dan turned to look at Jessie and then back to the girls and said, "What's the deal? Are you all planning on getting married, and you need to ask us for permission? What's the mystery?"

"Oh, Dad, be serious. This is very important to all of us."

"Okay, tell me what is so important and also so serious."

"Alicia, Bethany, and I are planning to go on a mission trip to Central America for two months. A missionary lady needs our help. She runs a small orphanage and mission for displaced women and children. She is badly in need of additional help. She had two ladies that were helping her, but one returned to her home in California. The other lady needs to go on furlough in order to satisfy the State Department's requirements for traveling abroad. She will be returning to the mission in two months."

"Is this something that the people here at Multnomah are suggesting that you do?"

This time Alicia answered. "The call came to the leaders here at Multnomah from the lady, Charlene Pearson, who is running the mission. She is a former graduate of Multnomah and has been in Guatemala for nearly fifteen years."

Jessie looked across to Mattie, now seated between her two friends, then to each of the girls and then let out a sigh. "Seems to me like the three of you have pretty well made up your minds to go on this mission. I need to ask you, Alicia and Bethany, have either of you talked to your parents about this?"

Alicia looked directly into Jessie's eyes and said, "My dad died when I was eleven. My mom has raised me. She believes that if the Lord is calling me on this mission, I should go."

Bethany stood up, stretched, and started to leave. Then, she turned back to face Jessie and said, "That was a hard push getting Mattie and that stupid car down the field. I am really tired. I think I had better head for my room."

Dan stood up and looked directly into Bethany's eyes. "What did your family have to say about your intentions pertaining to Guatemala, Bethany?"

"I don't have any family, Mr. Branson. I am an only child. Both of my parents were killed in an auto accident about three years ago. I am here on a full scholarship. Mr. Carl Guest, one of the officials here, has said that he and Mr. Peter Skaggs will pay all of my expenses if I decide to go on this mission."

Bethany and Alicia said their goodbyes and walked toward the door. Mattie sat still, staring at her parents, waiting for their response and comments pertaining to the proposal that had been made.

"I need to tell you that 'although' I am a firm believer in responding to the Lord's call, Mattie, I have strong feelings pertaining to the potential danger involved in this type of mission. Your mom and I don't want to encourage you to go on a mission that could cause you harm, either physically or emotionally."

"Dad, I trust you and Mom and your judgment. I really believe that the three of us will be blessed as we seek to serve the Lord in Guatemala. I know of your concerns. I wish I could talk to Angelo and see what he thinks."

"Sweetheart, God's angels appear when you need support. They don't hang around giving advice. If the Lord wants Angelo involved, He'll send him to you in a hurry."

"Mom, what are your feelings about all of this, and do I have your blessing?"

"Mattie, your dad expressed my feelings very well. If God wants you and your friends in Guatemala for two months, then I don't want to be the one to stand in your way. You know how much I love you, and I will promise you that because you are my baby, I will worry all the time you are there. I can assure you that I will be praying without ceasing that you will be safe. We all have to trust the Lord in these situations."

Mattie stood up from where she was seated on the couch facing her parents. At the same time, Dan stood up and held out his arms to his daughter. Jessie followed Dan's lead and went to her daughter, and the three of them stood hugging each other.

"I like your two friends. I hope you understand that your mom and I only want you to do what is in your heart. Could we possibly talk to Mr. Skaggs or Mr. Guest? Perhaps they can give us an insight as to what you three will be facing."

2

As the three entered the Administration Building, they were met in the hallway by Carl Guest, who was just leaving for the day. After listening a moment to Dan's request, he turned back towards his office. Carl suggested that Mattie take a seat in the hall outside of his office so that he could talk to her parents privately.

He entered his office, went behind the big desk, reached for the phone, and dialed a familiar number. A moment later, the side door opened, and Peter Skaggs entered with a broad smile on his face.

Following introductions, Peter looked at Dan and Jessie and said, "We've been expecting you two. Obviously, Mattie and her two friends have filled you in on where they want to be for two months.

"Multnomah School of the Bible has been responsible for sending hundreds of its students and graduates into pulpits and missionary assignments throughout the world.

"Mr. Branson, I have to tell you that we know quite a bit about you. I am aware that you are a dedicated Christian and that you have been called to serve the Lord on several occasions. We didn't hear this from your daughter but rather your reputation and some of your experiences are known by the staff and leadership here at Multnomah."

Jessie was looking over to Dan, anticipating a response to Peter Skaggs' comment. Dan did not comment. He smiled at both of the men and then reached for his wife's hand.

"The Lord has been very good to the Branson family. I need to tell you that I hold this institution in the highest regard. Mattie's mother and I were elated when our daughter advised us that she wanted to come to Multnomah. I know you are both aware that we have had Multnomah on our prayer list. Several times, the Lord has led us to provide financial support for many of your students that go into the mission field."

Peter and Carl were waiting for the Bransons to inquire about the mission in Guatemala. Dan had been studying the numerous photos pinned to the wall behind Carl's desk. He smiled, looked over at Jessie, and then turned to the two men.

"Gentlemen, I believe that both of you know that Guatemala has experienced quite a bit of unrest, especially during these past few years, even more so during these past few months. I know you are also aware that several State Department directives and news releases exist about the prevalent problems."

Jessie leaned forward in her chair and said, "My husband and I do not want to hold our daughter back, especially when she feels she is being called by the Lord to serve. We would like to know what your feelings are pertaining to the mission and the challenges they are about to assume."

Peter nodded to Carl, who cleared his throat, nodded his head slightly, and looked directly at Jessie.

"All we can tell you is that we are very familiar with Charlene Pearson. She attended Multnomah nearly fifteen years ago. She is a fine woman and has served her mission and the Lord faithfully for all of these years. We don't believe that she would seek our help if she did not believe that it was Gods' will."

Carl turned to Peter and said, "Peter, you know Charlene personally. What are your feelings about her request for help, and more importantly, how do you feel about Mattie, Alicia, and Bethany answering the call?"

"As Carl just said, Charlene is a very dedicated Christian lady. We have the highest regard for her. Furthermore, of all the students with whom I have come in contact here at Multnomah, I feel these three are the most qualified to answer Charlene's call for help.

"I have talked to each of the girls, and I have no doubt that they have their hearts set on going to Guatemala. They tell me they have studied the maps of the area and read everything they could get their hands on pertaining to the environment they are going to be exposed to. Apparently, all three of them took Spanish in their high school studies. I have been told that they all have a pretty good command of the Spanish language."

Dan stood up, held out his hand for Jessie and then turned to face the two gentlemen who had stood during the entire conversation. He put out his hand, first to Carl and then to Peter.

"Gentlemen, I am confident that you two are men of God. I know you would not endorse our daughters' desire to fulfill this mission unless you believed it to be the Lords' calling. Thank you for sharing your knowledge of this situation."

Dan pulled Jessie close to his side and looked into her face. She smiled at him and then nodded her assent to both Carl and Peter.

Carl spoke first, "Would you mind if we closed with a word of prayer?"

Dan and Jessie nodded their approval. As they stood there, they bowed their heads, continued to hold hands and listened as the two men prayed for the three girls. They also asked the Lord to give Dan and Jessie a peace in their hearts pertaining to the girls' safety. When the prayer ended, they thanked the two men, turned, and left the room.

Mattie, who had been sitting patiently on a single wooden chair positioned opposite the door, rose and watched as her parents walked towards her.

"You're going to have to call us every day. You have our blessing. Let's go home."

Mattie began to jump up and down and ran to hug each of her parents. They hugged for quite a while, and then Dan motioned for the two to follow him.

They exited the building, started down the long pathway, and headed in the direction of their rental car parked nearby.

Mattie stopped in the middle of the path and addressed both of her parents. "Mom, Dad, I asked Alicia and Bethany to spend a few days with us at the ranch. Is that okay?"

"That's fine with me, baby, but I think you should know that we are going to be busy with the cows. We will be heading them up the trail to the summer pasture this next week. If your friends come home with us, they will either have to join us on the trail or sit at the ranch house until we return. I need you with us on the trail."

At this time of year, the cows and all of their newborn calves would be herded up the trail and into the lush green pastures of the Cascades. An annual event, the drive would take nearly two days before they reached the plateaus and green meadows that would provide the herd with ample summer grazing.

"I knew that, Dad, and I told my friends that we have lots of horses and that maybe they could join the drive and help out."

"This is Friday. Do either of your friends have to be back on Monday?"

"No, some sort of conference or something with a bunch of missionaries is going on at Multnomah. We don't have any classes until next Thursday. You know, in just a few weeks, school will be out for the summer."

Dan looked at his daughter standing in front of them with a sparkle in her eyes. She wasn't jumping up and down anymore, and she was moving her shoulders from side to side waiting anxiously for her father's response.

"I would like to get back before dark. When will your friends be ready to go?"

"They're ready to go right now. If you look up at the second floor of the women's dorm, the third window from the left, you'll see them waiting for my signal."

Dan looked up to where Mattie was pointing and saw the two girls he knew to be Alicia and Bethany, both hanging out of the second floor window. They were waving their arms furiously.

Mattie stared at her dad with a questioning look. He looked at Jessie and then turned back to Mattie. He nodded his head OK as he looked at Jessie. She also nodded her approval.

Both Dan and Jessie knew that this would be a special time for Mattie and her two friends. It would be good for them to bond even closer and to strengthen them for the future that lay ahead in Guatemala. Their trip would require them to not only depend on each others' strength, but their individual spiritual commitments as well.

Mattie put a big grin on her face, turned, and jumped up and down, waving her arms at the same time. Immediately, the two figures disappeared and seconds later reappeared, running out of the front door toward the three of them.

When they caught up to the Bransons, they were both out of breath but grinning with exuberance. They were each gripping a small overnight bag. Clearly, they had counted on and were prepared in advance to join Mattie's family at their ranch in Sisters.

The group made their way to Dan's rental car, anticipating the next five days being an adventure and a time of spiritual strengthening.

3

Dan was speaking with the Flightcraft rental car agent as the four women walked out to the Bransons' Cessna 310 aircraft. The plane was parked in the transit parking area in front of the Flightcraft Executive Terminal on the east end of the Portland International Airport.

The turbo-charged, twin-engine plane carries six passengers with three rows of two seats. The aircraft was painted white with a bright metallic red design accenting the fuselage and wings. Just above the luggage door was a placard that read: Triple Peaks Ranch. Below the placard was the Triple Peaks brand, consisting of a '3' with a 'P' connected to the back spine of the '3.'

Dan never lost his love of flying. He learned the skills in the Air Force and had always maintained that the Air Force's training is the best in the world. Prior to the purchase of his present aircraft, he owned a Beechraft Bonanza. He loved his Bonanza; however, he had always been attracted to multi-engine aircraft.

When Dan had completed his rental car check-in, he walked out to the aircraft and found the four ladies standing beside the plane waiting for him.

They watched as Dan went through his pre-flight checklist and then motioned for the three girls to board the aircraft. Dan pointed at Mattie and told her to take the back seat. Mattie's two friends followed her in and took their seats in the second row.

Jessie waited until Dan had removed the wheel chocks and had climbed into the plane before she, too, climbed in and waited for Dan to close the door.

Inside the plane was total silence when Mattie, back in the third row, piped up: "Dad, Alicia has never flown before. Can you tell her to relax and that everything will be okay?"

"Sure, baby." Dan turned around and looked directly at Alicia, using his John Wayne imitation voice, he said, "Little lady, we're all going to do just dandy. If you see me taking a little snooze, you can just tap me on the shoulder, and I'll get right back to steering this here flying machine. Additionally, if you see me jump out of the plane wearing a parachute, please understand that I will only be going for help."

"Oh, great, Dad, that ought to make her feel just wonderful."

Following a taxi and takeoff clearance from the Portland control tower, Dan climbed to his cruising altitude and pointed the plane just to the right of Mount Jefferson, now looming into the clear, blue sky just ahead of them.

During his climb-out from the Portland airport, as directed, he switched his transponder code, showing that he was flying VFR (visual flight regulations) to his destination.

The late afternoon was spectacularly clear. Mount Hood was just a few miles to their left. Far off in the distance ahead, they could see the peaks of Mount Jefferson, the Three Sisters, Broken Top, and Mount Bachelor poking out of the mountainous terrain.

Dan turned to look at Alicia and noted that she had her nose pressed against her window. "How you doing there, little lady?"

"Mr. Branson, this is the most exciting thing I have ever experienced. This is truly beautiful. I never imagined it could be so spectacular to fly in a little airplane. I want to learn to fly so I can pilot my own airplane."

Everyone was chuckling at Alicia's decision to become a pilot and fly her own aircraft. Mattie leaned forward from her back seat and stuck her head between her two friends and began pointing out the various peaks on the horizon, some of them still showing a substantial amount of snow.

When his instruments indicated that he was 20 miles from the ranch, Dan lowered his altitude to a thousand feet above the terrain. He reduced power, lowered the landing gear, and slowly circled the ranch in order to provide Mattie's friends with a clear view of Triple Peaks Ranch and the looming mountains on the horizon to the west.

Mattie was excited as they flew over the ranch. She began to point out the different landmarks that showed her friends the area surrounding the ranch. As they flew over the ranch, she pointed out the main house, the three main barns, and the herd of cattle in the back pasture and the fields of alfalfa.

Following a smooth landing at the Redmond airport, they all climbed into the ranch's GMC Suburban and headed down the road to Sisters. As they pulled into the normal parking place for the suburban, Danny, Mattie's nearly thirteen-year-old brother, came out of the house and greeted his family. After, he was introduced to Alicia and Bethany, he then headed for the corrals to do his evening chores.

Mattie showed the girls to the big guestroom located on the main floor and told them that as soon as they had freshened up, they could go out and see the horses.

A few minutes later, the three girls made their way to the corral where Danny was busily feeding the horses. All three girls walked up and leaned over the corral fence.

"That great-looking, roan-colored horse over there by the back gate is mine. His name is Snickers. He is fourteen now. I got him when I was just six years old. I learned how to ride on another horse that we had called 'Lightning.' Lightning died a few years ago, and we buried him way out under the trees near the back of the pasture. I wish you could have met Lightning; he was a great horse.

"That's dad's horse, Sam, pushing all of the other horses away from the hay bin. He's really an old guy now, but he still wants the other horses to know that he is in charge. Danny's horse, Nugget, is the palomino standing beside Danny. He follows Danny everywhere he goes. Danny has a dog, too. His name is Barney. You can see him lying over there next to the tack room door. He's really pretty lazy and sleeps most of the day. He is a little over eight years old. He follows Danny like Nugget does and even comes in the house at night.

"I used to have a dog, too. She was a big St. Bernard named Heidi. She was really my best friend for a long time. When she died, she was nearly eleven years old. Dad and I buried her out in the corner next to Lightning."

"Wow, you have a lot of horses," Alicia said "Do you have names for all of them? Which ones are we going to get to ride?"

"Yes, they all have names. You and Bethany are going to get to choose your horses tomorrow; I'll help you. All together, we now have twelve horses. We're getting ready to take the herd up into the mountains this next week. Maybe Dad will let you help us.

"I think Dad is planning on flying us back to Multnomah next Wednesday. That gives us nearly five days to make our plans and enjoy the ranch."

Danny walked up to the fence, faced the girls, and leaned on the top rail. He had grown a little over six inches in the past two years and appeared to be on his way to standing well over six feet. He had a lot of his dads' features and mannerisms.

"I heard you girls talking. I think Dad will probably let you ride with us when we start the herd up to the mountain. You'll like it; it's a lot of fun.

"Did Mattie tell you that I plan to go to Multnomah as soon as I graduate? I'll be a freshman at Bend High School next year. I can hardly wait. I know a couple of friends who are planning to go there as well."

The girls and Danny chatted for a few minutes and then they began the walk across the pasture and back to the ranch house.

"Mattie, that's a big house you live in. It has huge windows in every room. You get a fantastic view of those giant peaks from every place in the house."

"That's true. When I was just a little girl and Mom and I met Dan, I thought maybe this place was just like heaven is going to be. Dan is the only dad that I have ever known.

"My real dad was killed in the war just a few months before I was born. God sent us to meet Dan. Actually, one of Gods' angels told us to come and meet him

"Mattie, that's a pretty strong statement to make. I have never met anyone who claimed to have actually talked to an angel. Did you see this angel or did you just hear his voice?"

"You know, I am not sure how you two will handle this, but I have to give it to you straight. He not only came to us like a real person, he also came by about six years later and had dinner with us."

Alicia and Bethany looked at each other. Unknown to Mattie, they both raised their eyebrows, indicating that they found Mattie's last statement very difficult to absorb. They were both still wearing a confused and questioning look when they walked into the mudroom adjoining the kitchen eating area.

"Hi, ladies. I saw you walking in from the corral. Alicia, you and Bethany look like you just saw a ghost. What has Mattie been telling you?"

"Not a ghost, Mrs. Branson. Mattie was telling us about meeting one of Gods' angels face to face."

"Oh, she must have been telling you about Angelo."

Jessie walked into the kitchen area with all three girls following close behind. She didn't seem to be concerned about Alicia's statement. She went about her task of preparing the evening meal. When she looked up, she saw both girls still standing there with their mouths open. Mattie had a smile on her face and was leaning against the countertop, looking out the window towards the mountains.

"I suppose Mattie and I should enlighten you two about Angelo. Let's go into the living room so that we can have a chat."

All four of them moved into the living room and sat down on the two facing couches. Mattie sat beside her mother, facing her two friends on the other couch.

"Let's see, where do I start? When Mattie was not quite six years old, we lived in Klamath Falls, about 180 miles south of here. Mattie was taking riding lessons from a very unhappy man. She wanted to quit and not take any more lessons. I took her to a local park and was trying to talk her into going back and finishing her lessons that I had already paid for. She cried and refused to go back. She was really being impossible.

"At that same time, an elderly gentleman came along and said he wanted to help me. I don't normally talk to strangers, but for some reason, I felt I should listen to this man. He talked to me, and then he handed me a letter and told me to come to Sisters and talk to Dan Branson. Mr. Angelo said that Dan was the best trainer in the area. I thought the letter was probably a letter of recommendation, but it turned out to be a personal letter about Mattie and me.

"The letter was written to Dan. He read the letter that told him that my husband, Mattie's father, was a passenger along with him when their vehicle was struck by a rocket in Iraq. Dan was the only survivor. My husband, Mattie's father, was killed instantly.

25

"Dan had previously experienced the presence of this very same person and knew him as Angelo. He advised Dan that he was indeed one of God's messengers. He told Dan to help us and teach Mattie how to ride.

"Mattie and I met Angelo again when he came about seven years ago and asked Dan to help a Christian rancher in Argentina. Actually, that very night, he stayed for dinner with our family.

"Yes, Alicia and Bethany, you two can be assured that this family has had the privilege of coming face to face with at least one of Gods' messengers."

Alicia and Bethany looked at each other and then both gave mother and daughter a big smile. They got up from where they were sitting and walked over to Jessie and Mattie, indicating that they wanted a hug.

Bethany spoke this time. "Wow, you two have experienced a wonderful blessing. God is really looking after all of you . . . actually your *whole* family. Have you met any other angels?"

"I think that is a question to ask Mr. Branson. I am sure he will surprise you with his answer. That is, of course, if he decides to tell you the whole story."

Again, the two exchanged glances. Jessie walked back into the kitchen to work on the evening meal. Mattie just smiled and said, "Do either of you need to wash up before dinner? I think Mom has just about got it ready to go on the table."

4

Dan was the last to take a seat at the dinner table. Since Matties' two friends made it six for dinner. Mattie was sitting beside her brother facing her two friends on the other side of the table. Dan sat at the head of the table, his normal position, and Jessie sat at the other end of the giant table that would easily accommodate twelve guests.

Mattie looked over at her father and saw him nod to her, indicating that she was to return the blessing. She reached out and grasped her mother's hand and then her brother's. As they all joined hands, Mattie bowed her head and thanked God for her home, her family, and her two friends. She completed her prayer by asking the Lord to watch over her and her two friends during the months to come.

Dinner was pot roast Dan's favorite. It also turned out to be a favorite for everyone as the large platter was nearly empty by the time dinner was over. Bethany and Alicia commented several times on Jessie's outstanding culinary skills. They referred to dinner as absolutely wonderful.

Danny said very little during the dinner. He was content to just listen to his sister and her two friends tell about their activities and experiences at Multnomah. When dinner had ended, Jessie suggested that everyone take a seat in the living room to enjoy dessert.

The living room seating arrangement had not been changed over the years. Two leather couches faced each other in front of the giant fireplace. Dan loved to refer to the fireplace as big enough to house a Volkswagen.

Dan and Jessie had their two leather chairs located at the end between the two couches, forming a 'U' shape facing the fireplace. A large wooden coffee table was in the center between the couches. A tall bronze statue of a mounted cowboy stood in the center of the table. Following the Bransons' purchase of the ranch, the Remington original bronze statue had been discovered in the basement—covered with many years of dust.

Three generations of the Henderson family were oblivious to the value of the art that had occupied the home for over a hundred years. Early in the last century, the patriarch of the family who built the big house purchased numerous pieces of art, including bronze statues and oil paintings.

The art pieces were discovered by Dan and Jessie shortly after they moved into the home. The discovery included several Charles Russell originals as well as numerous other famous western masterpieces hanging on the walls throughout the entire house.

The Henderson descendants were unaware of the value of the art pieces and left the entire collection behind. Pete and Gracie Henderson, the last of the family, sold the ranch to Dan and moved to southern Spain.

When everyone was seated in the living room, Jessie and Mattie served dessert, hot apple cobbler. Several oohs and aahs were heard as Mattie's two friends dove into their dessert.

Dan studied Bethany and Alicia as they placed their now empty dessert plates on the coffee table and leaned back on the couch. He was about to speak when Alicia leaned forward and looked him directly in the eyes.

"Mr. Branson, your wife and Mattie told us about Angelo. They said you had met him before, only he appeared to you as a woman. Will you tell us about meeting an angel?"

"Girls, I need to tell you that as you have probably heard, God works in mysterious ways. Although a Bible verse doesn't say that exactly, the Word does say,

"But we speak the wisdom of God in a mystery,
even the hidden wisdom, which God ordained
before the world unto our glory."
(1 Corinthians 2:7)

"I could tell you many stories about how the Lord has worked in my life as well as in the lives of many others. I believe the important thing for all three of you girls to remember is that when God calls you to His service, you can believe that He has a plan for you to accomplish His will. You can be assured that He knows of your needs."

"Mr. Branson, Alicia and I get the feeling that you have met many of God's messengers in your life. Can you tell us about your encounters?"

"I rely on one particular Bible verse. I am here now because of this Scripture."

"For he will give his angels charge over thee,
to keep thee in all thy ways."
(Psalms 91:11)

"If any of you ever begin to doubt God, just remember that verse and keep it close to your heart. I need to tell you that sometimes you may feel compelled to question God's timing; however, He is *always* faithful.

"A few times, I actually thought I had no way out of a situation that I got myself into. Without exception, He has always been faithful to come to my aid."

"Dad, why don't you tell Alicia and Bethany about meeting Michael?"

Bethany looked at Dan and said, "Really, the archangel Michael? Is that possible? Did you really get a chance to talk to him?"

"Well, he is quite a guy. He repaired my airplane engine when we were stranded in the mountains of Colorado. He even sprung me out of jail in Argentina. He has managed to be 'Johnnie-on-the-spot' whenever I really seemed to be in deep water over my head."

"Mr. Branson, why aren't more people experiencing meeting God's angels? Do you think that you are the only one, or do you believe that more people are just like you?"

"Hey, you three are the Bible students. You are asking me to quote the scriptures that you probably already know. The best way to answer your questions is to quote another verse that I am sure you have heard before."

"Be not forgetful to entertain strangers:
for thereby some have entertained angels unawares."
(Hebrews 13:2)

"Mattie's mom and I are excited for all three of you and your call to serve the Lord in Guatemala. My experience is that there are some very strong forces out there that are not going to want you to succeed. If you think that this is going to be a fun-filled experience, then I believe you are mistaken."

Jessie was watching all three of the girls' faces. She was holding back a great deal of pent-up emotions. Her past experiences told her that the girls were in for many challenges that they probably had not previously considered. "From a woman's perspective, I want you to know that as strong as you believe you are, you could very well be walking into a very difficult and stressful situation. Although each of you says that you have prayed about your calling, you will need to pray without ceasing. None of you have ever come face-to-face with the presence and power of the adversary."

"Mom and Dad, you two are scaring us to death. Can't you think positive about our calling? You need to give us credit for being smart enough to have weighed out all of the potential dangers that could face us."

"Baby, that's why your mother and I are talking to you this way. We not only give you credit for having thought things through, but we are very proud of all three of you for your commitment."

"Your dad is a pretty tough hombre," Jessie said, "and I have always believed I could handle just about any situation that confronted me, but my self-confidence has been challenged on several occasions."

"We're not trying to scare you. We're just trying to open your eyes to what could lie ahead of you. Your old dad is going to be nearly 3,000 miles away. You three are young, beautiful, and full of energy. We want you to stay that way."

Danny had been sitting, listening, and watching as the conversation between his folks, his sister, and her friends progressed. Finally, he stood up, stretched, and headed for the stairs to his bedroom. His dog Barney jumped up and began to follow his master.

"You people are giving me chills. I think I'll go upstairs to my room and read a book. Are we going to hit the trail early Monday morning, Dad? Are we going to let the girls come with us? Garrett says we need to start moving the herd first thing Monday. What do you think?"

"I think you ask too many questions. The answers to your questions are yes and yes. I agree with Garrett. Monday, we head them up and move them out. Go read your book, and you had better keep that hound off your bed."

5

Both Alicia and Bethany said their goodnights and went into the downstairs guest room. Although they both had stated that they were really tired, Dan and Jessie, who were watching the dwindling fire in the living room, could hear them talking and giggling for nearly an hour after they had entered the guest room.

The Saturday morning sunrise was visible from every window in the back of the Branson home and was casting a brilliant glow onto the snowcapped peaks of the western horizon.

Dan had walked to the tool shed to talk with Ron Morton, the ranch's foreman. He thought it strange that Ron would be working in the tool shed on a Saturday which was normally a day of very little work for Ron.

Ron was busily working on one of the wheels of the wind-rower machine. He was constantly working on the tractors and machinery that kept the farming end of the ranch going. He was totally responsible for every piece of machinery on the ranch.

"Howdy Ron, what have you got going? I didn't think I would find you out here on a Saturday working on machinery."

"I was just looking for something to do. I am not much of a sitter. I came out here so I could get this wheel on the wind-rower straightened out. I managed to hit the fence on one of my rounds this past year. I figured the time had come to get the thing back to the way it should be."

"Ron, Garrett is going to head the herd up the trail early Monday morning. We're all going to give him a hand. I'd like you to take care of the horses we'll be leaving behind. I expect we'll be coming back on Tuesday just before dark. We'll have Andy to drive the wagon, and Mattie's two friends from the Bible college will be lending a hand, too."

Andrew Gleason, whom everyone called Andy, was a retired sixty-eight-year old former Triple Peaks ranch hand. Andy was usually assigned to drive the wagon that contained all of the camping gear and food. This would be Andy's twentieth year working for Triple Peaks Ranch, driving the cattle to the summer range and assisting with the annual roundup.

"Sure, Boss, no problem. Hey, the alfalfa is looking good and so is the peppermint. I think we are going to have a great year. You can probably see that I have all the watering wheel lines going. They're expecting June and July to be pretty hot. I am really hoping to get three good alfalfa cuttings."

Dan thanked Ron and turned and walked back to the ranch house. As he entered the mudroom to hang up his vest, he saw Jessie walk into the kitchen eating area and set a bowl on the table. The room located between the mudroom and the kitchen turned out to be the most popular eating place for the entire family.

The pot-bellied stove in the room was radiating heat from the fiercely burning Tamarack wood that Jessie had loaded in earlier. A constant crackle was heard as wood burned inside the old-fashioned heater, making the room cozy and comfortable.

Not seeing Dan standing in the adjoining room, she went to the corner and opened the top of the Dutch door that lead out to the back of the house. She leaned out the door and addressed the three girls all leaning on the top rail of the fence. The girls were facing the snow-capped peaks enjoying the reflections made by the sunrise in the east.

"Okay, ladies, you can help put breakfast on the table. The guys will be in here in just a couple of minutes wanting a hot breakfast."

Jessie turned just as Dan stepped out of the mudroom, reached out and pulled her towards him. "Howdy, pretty lady, how about a smooch? You didn't see me hiding behind you, did you?"

He had startled Jessie. She gave him a scowl, a quick peck on the cheek, shoved him away, turned, and headed back to preparing breakfast. Dan smiled, nodded his head, and walked into the living room to take a seat in his leather chair.

The girls had finished setting the table and were in the process of taking their seats that faced the mountains when they saw Danny and Garrett coming in from the corral. They had fed and watered the stock, and as Jessie had commented, they were ready for the morning meal.

Jessie had already told the girls to set the table for seven, as she knew that Garrett would be joining them so that they could discuss the cattle drive. The girls were excited about participating in the drive and getting the herd started up the trail to the high country.

Following introductions, Garrett took his seat on the bench between Dan and Danny. The three men were across from the four women seated on the opposite side of the large harvest-style table. Alicia and Bethany were mesmerized by Garrett Sounders.

He was six-foot-four with a muscular build. He had an air about him that gave people comfort and assurance when he was in their presence. Only five years younger than Dan, he had long, black hair and wore a handlebar mustache that he felt gave him the appearance of a true character out of the Wild West.

He looked at the three girls sitting opposite him, smiled, and said, "Well, girls, what a real pleasure having you join us on our drive up to the summer pasture. Mattie has worked the herd before, so she will be in charge of keeping an eye on both of you."

"My plans are that we leave early on Monday. We can probably get to No Name Lake, an easy four-hour trail ride from the ranch.

"We're going to have to keep the herd moving pretty steady to make it there. I calculate that we will need about eight hours in order to arrive before dark. Driving cattle is much slower than just riding up a trail. If all goes well, we'll have the herd to where I want them by noon on Tuesday."

The three girls looked at each other and then back to Garrett. They were extremely excited!

After breakfast, Garrett thanked Jessie for the meal and indicated that he had much to do before they would be heading the herd up the trail on Monday morning.

As he started to leave the mudroom, he turned and faced Mattie. "You ought to take your friends down to the corral and fix them up with a couple of horses. I would recommend you hook them up with Dusty and Zipper. Although neither of them has been ridden for a while, they both know the trail and the routine.

"You might also consider saddling up and taking your friends up the trail for a couple of hours sometime before Monday morning. You'll want them to get used to the saddle. I figure I will see you all in church tomorrow if I don't see you again today."

The two girls had their eyes glued to the handsome cowboy as he exited the room and headed up the path leading to the corral.

Alicia spoke first. "Wow, that is one fascinating man. He looks like he just jumped out of a time machine from the old west. How old is he?"

"He's much too old for any of you. He's just a few years younger than Mattie's dad," Jessie said as she motioned for the girls to help clear the table and take the dishes into the kitchen.

"Why don't you gals head out to the corral and get acquainted with your horses. If you are going to saddle up and go for a ride, then be sure to be back by three. I want all of you to go into town with me. I have to pick up the food for the two days' ride.

"Mattie, you should pack a lunch if you're going to take your friends for a trail ride. Maybe you three can help me plan the menus. I calculate that we will have two lunches, two dinners and two breakfasts. I believe Dan plans to fly you girls back to Portland Wednesday afternoon."

Mattie made up three quick lunches and then led her two friends down the path to the corral. Once they were in the corral, she motioned for them to take up positions next to the tack room. Twelve horses were bunched together near the water tank. All of them, except Sam, turned as she walked towards them.

"Okay, guys and gals, get out of my way. I just want Snickers, Zipper, and Dusty. The rest of you just move aside."

She pushed her way in between the horses and began to shove them aside as she grabbed the halters on the three to which she had referred.

The horses that had been selected to make the trail drive were left with their halters on. The rest were expected to head out of the open gate to graze in the south pasture.

Snickers, Zipper, and Dusty obediently followed her as she led them to the hitching rail in front of the tack room. She clipped lead ropes onto each of their halters and then tied them to the hitching rail.

Mattie introduced each of them to their horses. She directed Alicia to Zipper and then Bethany to Dusty. Mattie turned and walked toward the tack room. She didn't turn her head as she spoke loud enough for both to hear. She had previously said the girls could choose their horses, but now she wasn't going to leave that to chance.

"Get acquainted with those two horses. They're going to be your transportation for two days. If you don't show them that you like them, they can make your life miserable while we're on the trail."

A few minutes later, Mattie reappeared in the open doorway and motioned for her two friends to join her inside. She directed each of them to saddles that were situated side-by-side on saddletrees protruding from the wall.

Motioning again for them to follow her, she grabbed two of the three saddles she would need and their blankets and walked toward the two horses. She motioned for Alicia to grab the other saddle, her saddle, and follow her out the door. She placed a blanket on each of the horses' backs and then grabbed each one of the saddles and in one single motion placed it squarely in the middle of the blanket.

The two girls were mesmerized by Mattie's smooth and experienced actions. Both girls' eyes were glued on Mattie, waiting for the next command.

When she had finished cinching up each of the saddles and was confident that they were rigged properly, she motioned once again for the two girls to follow.

Mattie turned to the two following close behind her and pointed to a large rectangular box located in the back corner of the tack room. She had always referred to the box as the boot coffin.

"Look through the boots in that big box and pick out a pair that fit. Don't worry about how fancy they look. You want them to fit well as you'll need to be comfortable while you're in the saddle. Remember, you're going to be wearing them constantly for two days."

The two girls scurried over to the 'boot coffin' and began to try on riding boots. They were giggling as they discovered many that were too big and an equal number that were too small.

Finally, Mattie, holding three bridles in her hands, observed them standing next to each other, smiling and displaying their choices. She nodded her approval and motioned for the girls to follow.

While she was putting the bridles in each of the horse's mouths, she explained their known personalities. She pointed out that Zipper always liked to be in front, and, quite the opposite, Dusty was content with just following.

Satisfied that her two friends were properly oriented, she quickly mounted Snickers and settled back into her own, very familiar saddle. Alicia and Bethany quickly followed, both having broad smiles and looks of excited anticipation on their faces.

Mattie set the pace just below a trot. She wanted the girls to experience as much of the trail as possible and get used to their saddles. They would be spending hours in the saddle during the next few days, and she knew she had to get them used to their saddles and riding.

Despite the rigor of learning how to ride, Mattie's two friends managed to do very well. They were constantly chatting back and forth, talking about school, boys, and their recent car-pushing race. The activities at Multnomah are limited, as the curriculum is demanding and provides very little leisure time.

The day was spectacularly beautiful. The snow-capped peaks that jutted the skyline to the west had a majestic appearance that, as the girls remarked, literally took their breath away. A light breeze joined them as they followed the well-marked trail that led into the mountains.

They could hear the sounds of chipmunks chattering and the light breeze blowing through the branches of the giant Ponderosa pines. The sounds gave off a tranquilizing effect as the girls guided their horses up the winding trail.

6

Nearly two hours had passed by, quickly, time consumed by continuous chatter, chuckles, and occasionally very loud laughter. The three seasoned quarter horses were accustomed to the trail. This particular trail was not only familiar to the horses, but also to Mattie.

"Hey, you two, I think that Snickers has something, maybe a small rock, stuck in his front right hoof. I am going to stop and check it out. You two head on up the trail. Just around the bend you will see a picnic table and a fire pit. Give your horses a rest, and I'll be along in a couple of minutes."

Alicia and Bethany shrugged their shoulders, nodded to each other, and continued the slow pace up the trail and around the bend.

Mattie jumped down and walked around to the front of her horse. She carefully lifted his right hoof and began to inspect the bottom, looking for whatever was causing him to falter.

"Hey, partner, you got a hunk of something stuck in your hoof. Hang tight while I get some tools from my saddle bag."

She rummaged through the saddlebag and finally retrieved a husky pair of wire cutters. Wire cutters were considered an absolute essential for anyone challenging the mountain trails. Coming across lengths of barbed wire that had somehow been discarded by previous riders, or sometimes poachers, was not unusual.

Mattie worked skillfully on the sharp object lodged in Snickers' hoof. It turned out to be a long piece of shale that had more than likely broken off of a large rock.

She completed her task in less than five minutes and climbed back on Snickers, settling into her saddle and nudging her horse up the trail in order to rejoin her friends.

As she rounded the bend in the trail that led to the small picnic area, she was amazed when she saw Alicia and Bethany still sitting in their saddles, facing the picnic table. Only a portion of the table was visible as she rode up to her two friends.

Alicia and Bethany had stopped their horses a few feet from the table. The two horses were only inches apart and seemed to be taking in the surroundings without any concern. The girls were both sitting up straight in their saddles, staring at the picnic table. They both appeared rigid with fear.

Mattie led Snickers up beside Bethany's horse, Zipper, and looked over to the picnic table. She let out a squeal as she jumped down from Snickers, let the reins fall to the ground, and literally leaped at the man who had been sitting on the bench.

The man was roughly in his late fifties, stood about five-foot-ten and was wearing a bow tie. He was dressed in a brown tweed three-piece suit and had a broad smile on his face and a sparkle in his eyes as he hugged Mattie.

Mattie turned to her two friends with streams of tears pouring down her face as she jumped up and down like a little child. She could hardly contain herself.

"Get down you two. You've got to meet one of my very best friends."

Alicia and Bethany gave each other a confused and almost frightened look as they followed Mattie's instructions and dismounted. The two stood close together as they walked hand in hand to where Mattie stood, gripping Angelo's hand.

"Ladies, this man standing here in this funny looking suit is none other than the person Mom and I told you about. This is Angelo. If you remember, we all studied some Greek this past year at Multnomah. You should remember that Angelo in Greek means 'messenger.'"

Mattie turned back to look at Angelo and studied his attire. He was dressed in a fashion familiar to the mid-1950s.

Noticing Mattie examining his attire, he responded, "The middle years of this last century were some of my favorite years. People were not as frantic and demanding as they are now in the twenty-first century. People dressed up more, and this particular outfit is one of my favorites."

All three girls were now standing in front of Angelo with Alicia and Bethany unusually close to each other.

"Mattie, are you trying to tell us that this man standing here is one of God's angels? He doesn't look like an angel," Alicia stated with a questioning look on her face.

Angelo spoke in a soft, yet reassuring voice. "You must be Alicia Clark, Bob and Carole's daughter. You really do resemble your mother. Your parents both love you very much. They are extremely proud of what you are doing with your life."

Angelo turned slightly and faced Bethany. "Your dad, Frank Thomas, asked me to give you this." With that, he stepped forward and hugged the young woman. Tears were now streaming down all of their faces. Angelo not only appeared to them, but he brought with him a semblance of love from Alicia's and Bethany's parents, who had been called to be with the Lord.

Mattie commented that Angelo had not changed in appearance since her first encounter nearly thirteen years earlier in the city park in Klamath Falls, Oregon. Angelo just smiled and said, "Some things never change."

Mattie looked over to the horses and motioned for the girls to follow her lead as she walked her horse over to a small tree and attached Snickers' lead rope to one of the lower branches. Both girls followed suit and then turned to accompany Mattie back to where Angelo was still standing.

All three let out a gasp as they saw Angelo dressed in blue jeans and a sweatshirt emblazoned with the words, "He Lives". He had a big grin on his face.

"Wow, you are some quick-change artist, Angelo. I haven't seen you in that outfit before. I love it. Now you look like one of us," Mattie said.

"I thought maybe you would feel more comfortable if I switched into a more appropriate outfit."

As they approached Angelo, he motioned for them to take seats on the opposite side of the table so that they could all face him and absorb what he had to say. He had a message for the girls.

"I have been sent here to tell you things you need to know about where you are going.

"First, you need to know that this isn't going to be just a fun trip to Central America. Guatemala is known to be one of the most wicked and evil areas on the face of the earth. Although many born-again Christians live in Guatemala, they are a very small minority. As you know, true followers of Christ are in many of the Christian denominations.

"I think I should emphasize that you are going to be facing frightening circumstances. Many of the locals do not like the idea of an evangelical mission, such as that being run by Charlene Pearson. As you have been told, it is also a women's refuge and an orphanage. Charlene and her assistants have been presenting the Gospel to all of the kids on a daily basis. Several decisions have been made for Christ, and He has touched many young lives.

"I know that I am telling you things that you probably have already heard or have guessed. However, I must emphasize that you all need to pray constantly during your stay with Charlene Pearson. She is a very strong woman of faith and has also been tested many times. You will all do well to follow her example."

Alicia was staring down at the tabletop. She looked up into Angelo's eyes and searched his face, looking for some hint of fear. All she could see was calm and a look of confidence as he talked.

"Will you be there to protect us if things go wrong? Can we depend on you to keep us out of harm's way?" she asked.

"Ladies, the Lord has placed limits on his messengers. We can't just go into a situation and dictate the outcome. You will be on your own in Guatemala. Remember, God's will has always been that none should perish.

"Furthermore, He has promised that He will never leave you nor forsake you; however, you must depend on God's Holy Spirit to lead you each moment of every day. As I mentioned earlier, you must pray constantly and depend on Him to show you the way."

Angelo spoke to them for nearly an hour. Silence had overtaken all three girls. Each of them were either staring at the sky, the tabletop, or the surrounding scenery. Angelo's words had a sobering effect on the three of them.

"I think the three of you should return to the ranch. You probably have lost track of time, but we have been talking for almost an hour. Mattie, your dad or Garrett will be heading up the trail looking for you if you don't get moving. Aren't the three of you also supposed to help Jessie with the shopping? The most important advice I can give you is to remember that God is with you always."

The three girls started to rise from their seats when Angelo motioned for them to stay sitting.

"I would like us to have a word of prayer. I think each one should pray and ask God to bless your mission to work with Charlene Pearson."

Tears were running down the cheeks of all three of the girls when they completed their prayers. They had no doubt that their Father in Heaven had heard their petitions.

Angelo looked at the tear-streaked faces. With a big smile and a sparkle in his eyes, he said, "I love seeing 'Holy Water' at a time like this."

As soon as the three girls arrived back at the ranch and had taken care of their horses, they rushed into the big house. They found Dan and Jessie sitting in front of the mammoth fireplace discussing the upcoming cattle drive to the summer range.

Within a matter of seconds, Mattie's parents surmised that something special had taken place on their afternoon ride. The girls' faces were all smudged as if they had been crying. They both looked at Mattie and waited for her to tell them what was causing her to be bouncing in her seat on the big leather couch.

"He was on the trail, Mom and Dad. Just like before; he came out of nowhere and met us at the new picnic area on the trail. He told us all about our mission, and then he told Alicia and Bethany about their parents. What an awesome experience! He is the most wonderful man I've ever met. I guess I should say angel, because that is who he really is."

"Sounds like our friend Angelo has made an appearance," Dan said as he leaned forward in his big chair. "Did he say you three were going to be enjoying a fantastic vacation in Central America?"

"No, Dad, he said that we needed to pray a lot because Guatemala is a wicked place. He assured us that our trip was not going to be easy serving with Charlene Pearson."

The five of them chatted about Angelo, and then the girls' started to plan their trip to Guatemala, for nearly an hour.

Finally Dan indicated that he needed to go out and meet with Garrett. He wanted to review the plans and details of the upcoming drive. He stood up and reached for Jessie's hand and then, with his other, he grasped the hand of his teenage son.

"I'd really like to take a moment to pray and thank God for sending his messenger, Angelo, to talk to you three girls."

Dan bowed his head and proceeded to thank the Lord for blessing the Branson family, as well as Mattie's two friends from Multnomah.

When Dan had finished his prayer, Jessie turned to the girls and said, "Get a move on, ladies. We have to go get some grub for the next two days."

* * *

The Sunday morning service at the little non-denominational church located on the outskirts of the small western town of Sisters began promptly at 11 am. The church was packed full for the morning worship. Bob Seeley, the pastor, had called everyone that he knew advising them that the Bransons' daughter and two of her friends were about to embark on a two-month mission to Guatemala.

The preacher's sermon was based on the sixteenth chapter of Mark. As he ended his sermon, he looked directly at the three young ladies, sitting together in the third row, and quoted from memory:

"And they went forth, and preached everywhere,
the Lord working with them, and confirming the word
with signs following."
(Mark 16)

7

Monday morning's sunrise was breath-taking. The deep, blue sky was crystal clear. The early morning had a familiar pink glow on the majestic skyline. Jessie woke the girls at the crack of dawn and told them that breakfast would be on the table in fifteen minutes.

Bethany and Alicia sleepily looked at each other, shrugged their shoulders, and decided that applying makeup and primping in front of the bathroom mirror would not be an option.

When the two entered the kitchen, they found Mattie and her mom busy placing steaming hot food onto the big harvest table. Again, the table was set for seven. A moment later, Garrett entered the kitchen and addressed Jessie in a condescending tone of voice.

"Jess, I have the wagon all loaded. Can you imagine that I managed to get all the food you bought into only one wagon?"

Jessie scowled at Garrett and said, "You like to eat as well as the rest of us. Don't complain about my menus or how much grub you had to load unless you want to do all the cooking."

Jessie placed an oversized platter of pancakes in the middle of the table and sat down. Mattie brought in two platters, one heaping with bacon and the other an equal-sized platter of fried eggs.

As everyone was now seated, they all looked to Dan to ask the Lord's blessing. Just as he was about to bow his head, Bethany looked around the table and then spoke in a soft voice.

"Mr. Branson, may I return the blessing this morning? I really feel like God has blessed Alicia and me with all that we are experiencing. I want Him to know how much we love Him."

"Please do, Bethany. Our family is very happy that you and Alicia have joined with Mattie on this Central America mission."

Everyone grasped the hand next to them and held firmly as Bethany asked the Lord to continue to bless the Branson family and watch over everyone as they drove the herd from the ranch up into the mountains to the summer pastures. She closed her prayer by thanking the Lord for what she described as a scrumptious breakfast.

Following breakfast, Garrett, who had for the past five years been the head wrangler for the Triple Peaks Ranch, gathered everyone together in order to explain their specific duties. He assigned each person a special position with the herd. The cattle head count was just over one hundred cows and 114 calves.

Garrett explained that the biggest job would be to keep the calves in with the herd, as they always liked to wander. Dan was chosen to lead the herd. Garrett asked Alicia and Bethany to join Dan at the head of the herd. Jessie and Mattie were experienced in the drive and were assigned to the flanks of the herd keeping them close to the trail.

Garrett had put the two girls with Dan for several reasons. The first reason was that neither of the girls were experienced riders. Additionally, getting caught between some of the moving cattle can sometimes be very frightening and dangerous. Cattle that are being herded are, for the most part, being moved against their will. The herd is normally stubborn and moves only when it is forced.

Garrett took a position at the very end of the herd, commonly known as the "drag." Danny was assigned to work the trail behind the herd, keeping a sharp eye out for stragglers and wandering calves. Danny would be galloping from one side to the other, constantly looking for and chasing the stragglers back into the herd.

Andy would leave thirty minutes before the herd was headed up the trail. He was expected to have most of the camp set up when everyone else arrived at the lake.

Without any rain for several days, the trail and the surrounding grounds were very dry. As the herd moved up the trail, the dust became almost unbearable. About that time, Dan turned and rode up beside the two girls.

"I believe I should tell you young ladies that the reason you always see a cowboy with a neckerchief is so that he can cover most of his face when working a herd. You'll quickly find out that it keeps out most of the dust."

Immediately, he pulled his neckerchief up and over his mouth and nose. The girls followed his lead and did the same. Dan motioned for Bethany and Alicia to take the lead as he turned Sam back toward Jessie to see how well the herd was staying together.

Jessie signaled with a thumbs-up that she had her side under control. She gave Dan a salute and waved him to the other side of the herd. She had most of her face covered with her neckerchief and her hat pulled down tight in front. She wore extra large dark glasses that reminded Dan of a familiar comic strip character. He knew he could never share that opinion with his wife, though.

Jessie became quickly accustomed to the requirements of getting the herd either up to the summer pastures or back down to the ranch in the fall. Actually, she had not only become accustomed to the requirements of herding the cattle, but she enjoyed it.

When Dan broke through the herd to the other side, Mattie could not be seen in either direction. They were on a long straight stretch in the trail, and he wondered what had happened to her. He was a little anxious as he sat in the saddle, motionless, watching the herd move up the trail.

Suddenly, two cows and two calves came bursting through the trees with Mattie close behind, swinging her lariat and yelling at the top of her voice. He felt a rush of pride as he observed his daughter skillfully weaving between the trees, pushing the stragglers back into the herd.

Dan finally made his way to the back of the herd and saw Garrett with his face and clothing covered with dust. Garrett saw Dan coming and he, too, gave a thumbs-up signal that meant all was going well.

About that time, both men saw Danny and his horse, Nugget, pass behind the herd on a dead run. He was hot on the trail of a couple of strays.

The sun was beginning to sink below the giant, rugged peaks to the west when the herd finally reached No Name Lake. With little effort, they got them assembled near the small lake. Eager for the water, they managed to nearly surround the lake. After drinking their fill of the fresh mountain water, they settled down and began to graze on the sweet grass near the water's edge.

Garrett announced that Danny would take the first four-hour shift at 8:00 pm to keep the herd together and quiet. He planned to relieve Danny at midnight, and then Dan would take over at four in the morning.

Jessie, the girls, and Andy Gleason were placed in charge of finishing the camp set-up and preparing the evening meal. Andy would get a fire started while the girls would attend to the dinner. Following the next morning's breakfast, the whole team would pitch in to break camp, load the gear back onto the wagon, and get Andy started up the trail.

All of the girls, including Jessie, stated that following dinner and the clean up, they would be going to the opposite end of the lake to take a dip. The guys just looked at each other, shrugged their shoulders, and nodded that they understood.

"Are you all going to skinny dip?" Danny asked with his eyes staring intently at his mom.

"Hardly. We got a ton of dirt on us and our clothes. I can't wait to get most of it off in the water."

"Be prepared for a little environmental shock when you jump into the water. The best spot is near the other end of the lake with a big rock where the water is only about four feet deep. Remember, the water in this lake is still mighty cool," Dan said.

The four men sat around the fire talking about the herd and the drive. They had brushed the dust from their clothing and were perfectly satisfied with their appearance, and none of them had any intention of jumping into the frigid waters of this little alpine lake.

Later, when the ladies got back to the camp soaking wet in their clothing, they huddled around the fire and attempted to dry out and get warm.

"You were right, dear husband; the water in this lake is mighty cold. We all brought along dry clothes, but I think we will just stand here and absorb some of the heat from this fire for a few minutes."

Ten minutes later, the girls finally stopped shaking from the cold. Having warmed up, they headed for their tents to change into dry clothes. The last thing any of them needed was to catch a cold or get sick while on the drive.

A total of three tents were set up near the campfire. Garrett and Danny shared a tent, and Dan and Jessie also had their own tent. The three girls all shared a larger tent. Andy rolled out his sleeping bag underneath the wagon and claimed he had the best accommodation.

A short time later, the ladies returned to the campfire dressed in dry clothing and wearing smiles.

The evening meal had consisted of meat loaf, corn, and mashed potatoes prepared by Jessie the day before. She had also thrown in two of her famous frozen apple pies that managed to thaw out during the drive. Everyone agreed that the whole meal was incredibly good and would last them until morning.

The evening was cool, but not cold. The sun had long since set, and the sky was beginning to fill with millions of blinking stars. Everyone was enjoying the campfire and making small talk about the day's drive when Andy walked up with a harmonica. He sat down on one of the logs that had been drug up to the fire and began to play familiar songs such as "He's Got the

Whole World in His Hands." Together, they all sang song after song with some imperfect harmonizing. Finally, Andy held up one finger signifying that the next would be his last song. He finished the evening's sing-along by softly playing the inspiring sounds of "Kumbaya." Far off in the distance, Dan could hear his son, Danny, who was watching the herd, loudly singing along with them.

Alicia and Bethany, totally exhausted, stood up, said their goodnights, and headed for their respective sleeping bags. As they walked to their tent, it was obvious that they were both nursing very tender parts of their bodies as well as sore muscles. Mattie, with a knowing smile on her face, watched her two friends limp to their tent. She stood up, bent and kissed her mom and dad goodnight, and then headed for her tent.

Dan continued to sit by the fire. Using a long steel rod, he patiently continued moving the remaining logs into one pile in the middle of the dwindling fire. Jessie moved over beside Dan and leaned against his shoulder. "We truly have been blessed, haven't we?" she murmured into his ear.

Dan nodded his agreement. The two sat silently mesmerized by the fire for several more minutes before they decided to go to their tent.

Just as they were about to get up, Jessie leaned over towards Dan, planted a kiss on his ear, and said, "I sure do love you, cowboy. You have made me the happiest woman in the whole wide world."

The stillness of the rest of the night was occasionally interrupted by Andy's heavy snoring or the bleeping cry of a calf that had wandered away from its mom.

Dan and Jessie walked hand-in-hand to their tent. Once they were alone, they moved into each other's arms and held each other tightly. Finally Dan said, "I've got a short night ahead of me. I have to get up and relieve Garrett at four." Within a couple of minutes, Dan began to breathe deeply.

Jessie was wide awake for a long while. She thought about her life and what had taken place over the past thirteen years. She could hardly believe how she had been so blessed. She had truly loved Bob Hart and honestly thought she could never love again when he was killed in Iraq.

When God—actually his angel, Angelo—came to her, she had no idea that God's plan was that she could once again experience so much love.

Now, the Lord was calling her daughter into one of the world's most dangerous places: Guatemala.

Jessie closed her eyes and began to repeat the same prayer that she had been making daily since Mattie and her friends had advised them of their plans to work at a mission in Central America.

8

As per his instructions from the previous evening, Garrett was awakened at 7 am. This time, he had only received about three hours sleep, as he had been on watch from midnight until 4 am. However he felt good as he had logged about four hours sleep when he hit the sack shortly after dinner.

Dan and Garrett both had managed nearly a full night's sleep. Garrett felt refreshed and looked forward to heading back to the ranch.

When he climbed out of his tent, he could smell the tantalizing aroma of bacon. As he walked up to the campfire, Jessie handed him a steaming cup of coffee, a plate heaped with French toast, and a rasher of bacon. He moved over to the makeshift work table, set his coffee down, and poured a large amount of maple syrup on his plate with a big hunk of butter. Then stood by while Jessie flopped two over-easy eggs on top of his French toast. She knew exactly how he liked his breakfast.

He turned and took a seat on the big log beside the fire. The fire that had been roaring an hour ago was now beginning to die down and would soon be completely doused with water prior to their leaving the campsite.

Consistent with his usual practice, he gulped his food, trying to consume the entire breakfast in record time. After handing his empty plate to Mattie, he burped, wiped his chin and mustache with the back of his sleeve, pulled his long hair back, and grinned at

Mattie. She returned his grin with a scowl and uttered a "Yuk" at his crude behavior. He grinned again.

"Great chow, boss ladies. By the way, did either of you hear the rain in the night? I don't think we got very much, but it might be enough to settle the dust. I know I didn't imagine it because I felt it coming down when I was on watch."

He refilled his cup with fresh coffee and sauntered over to where Dan was in the process of loading a few remaining items into Andy's wagon.

When Andy finished his breakfast and the last few drops of coffee in his cup, he handed the empty plate and cup to Mattie, thanked the women for breakfast, and walked over to join Dan and Garrett by the wagon.

Danny walked over to where the three men were standing to listen to their conversation. He had just completed hitching the team to Andy's wagon.

The men were discussing the condition of the herd. They agreed that the herd had stayed calm throughout the night and were grazing on the sweet grass, close to the lake. Garrett mentioned that he felt the rain for a little while around two in the morning.

"I think we can get the herd to our regular drop area by midday. I know you want to get back to the ranch before sunset. Andy will stay with the herd until Saturday when those two young guys, Craig Terrell and Mark Carmine, who worked for us last summer, show up. They were good men and did well this past year. I know we can count on them to take care of the herd." Garrett said.

"I agree," Dan said. "I think that by the looks of things here at the camp, we should be able to push the herd back onto the trail in less than an hour. If we can keep that schedule, we can make the ranch before sunset.

"Mildred stayed at the house last night and took care of Barney. Ron is looking after the stock that we left behind. I know Mildred likes housekeeping better than taking care of Danny's dog. She'll be glad to see us ride back in before sunset.

"Barney will be happy to see Danny. I told him that his dog would have to stay at home this time. That crazy little dog loves to chase squirrels and chipmunks. I was afraid that he would forget where he was and dash under the feet of the moving herd. We all had a hard enough time when Heidi, Mattie's dog, died. I don't want to go through that kind of grief for a while."

Jessie walked over to where the men were standing by the wagon. She stood there for a minute until Dan stopped talking.

"Guys, I think we're all packed and ready to hit the trail. The girls are getting saddled up and should be ready in about twenty minutes."

"Okay, boss lady. Andy, you had better grab those last few things over by the fire pit, load them into your wagon, and start up the trail. I plan on turning the herd loose in that big grassy meadow just past the fork to Red Meadows," Garrett commented as he turned toward Andy and pointed at the three boxes sitting near the smoldering campfire.

Andy placed the last few items into the wagon, climbed onto the driver's seat, and looked at Garrett.

"Okay to hit the trail, Garrett? I think I am fully loaded, and the team looks like they're ready to go. I'll go ahead and pitch a camp just beyond the Red Meadows fork."

Garrett didn't respond verbally, he just pointed to the trail and waved for Andy to go. He, Dan, and Danny stepped back from the side of the wagon and watched as it began to move out and onto the trail. He agreed they would need another thirty minutes before they would be able get the herd assembled and moving back up the trail.

The herd was not anxious to leave the sweet grass that had been available to them for past several hours. With a lot of shrill whistling, outright yelling, and a substantial amount of force, the herd was convinced to finally move. Garrett actually pushed his way into the lingering herd and slapped quite a few of them on the rump with his lariat.

Dan looked up the trail from where he was sitting on Sam's back and could see an occasional puddle, indicating that Garrett was right about the rain shower in the middle of the night. Jessie had commented that she, too, had heard the same thing.

Finally, the seven riders were able to get the entire herd back on the trail moving up towards their summer pasture. They were moving slowly, but they were moving. Once Garrett was confident that the whole herd was accounted for, he began to urge them into a slightly faster pace.

Everyone noticed a conspicuous absence of dust as the herd moved forward. The nighttime showers had settled the dust, making the whole drive much easier for Garrett and Danny, who were again positioned at the back of the herd. Danny began to cross back and forth across the trail, making sure no stragglers existed.

Garrett kept urging the herd forward, never allowing any of them to stop and graze.

In four short hours, they reached the spot where Andy had stopped the wagon and set up camp. He had a small fire going and had already positioned his bedroll under the wagon. Dan's watch indicated the time was a few minutes before one in the afternoon.

Jessie tied her horse beside Andy's wagon and began digging through the boxes. In only a couple of minutes, she came up with the ingredients to prepare a lunch for everyone. Dan suggested that they eat while riding down the trail heading for the ranch. He calculated that with their steady pace, they would reach the ranch in five hours.

Andy unhitched the team from the wagon. He led one of the horses to Garrett's horse and tied the horse's lead rope to the back of Garrett's saddle. He led the other horse over to a small tree and tied him to a protruding branch. Andy had his saddle in the wagon. Tomorrow, he would saddle the horse and ride out into the herd and Garrett would take the other horse back to the ranch.

Dan and Danny walked out among the herd, watching the cows and the calves reunited now that the drive had ended. Most of the cows had made this trek in previous years and were familiar with the summer pastures.

"The grass up here really looks good this year, Dad. I think the herd will really do well through the summer, don't you?"

Dan looked at his son standing tall beside him. He thought of how much he had been blessed during the last several years. He studied Danny and was sure he was going to grow into a strong man, serving the Lord just as he had been called to do. Dan's dream was that someday Danny would go off to college and then return to take over the Triple Peaks Ranch.

"You're right, Son. The meadows will stay this green most of the summer. The rain showers will bring the short grass back to where it was before the grazing began. Each critter requires about ten acres in these mountains, but the grass is sweet, and they'll do well.

The ladies took a few minutes to whip up a lunch bag for each person. They made ham and cheese sandwiches. Alicia and Bethany walked around and handed each person a bag containing the sandwich as well as cookies, an apple, and a bottle of water. After returning the leftover food to the wagon storage container, Jessie climbed into her saddle and motioned for the girls to follow suit. They did not hesitate. Actually, Mattie's two friends were beginning to look and act like seasoned trail riders!

Dan looked around and was satisfied that all would be well with the herd. Andy was very dependable and loved what he was doing. Now the time had come to head back down the trail.

Jessie and the girls took the lead while Dan, Garrett, and Danny followed. Dan had stated that they needed to maintain a pretty good pace in order to make the ranch before sunset. None of them were excited about riding the mountain trails after dark. Everyone gave a wave to Andy, and the group moved out.

The ride back to the ranch was uneventful. They stopped for five minutes every hour in order to let the horses rest. The tall grass that was pretty well trampled down the day before now looked like it hadn't been touched due to the refreshing rain of the night before.

The two men discussed all of the things that needed to be done at the ranch. Danny's head was constantly moving back and forth. He was looking for just about anything, bird or critter, that had taken up residence in this area of the woods.

Dan commented that Ron had indicated that the alfalfa was doing well and how he estimated that this year's crop would yield at least two tons per acre. This meant that the two hundred acres of alfalfa would yield nearly four hundred tons of high-grade, 18 percent protein hay.

He pointed out that the peppermint would do much better if the days would warm up. The mint grew much faster when they days were hot and the sun high in the sky. Everything would be harvested and distilled just prior to bringing the herd down from the mountains this coming fall.

The oil would be stored in the round barn until he and his buyers would agree on a price. They needed to keep the oil stored in the barn until a fair price could be reached. Dan knew that he was fortunate in that he wasn't forced to sell his oil at the end of the season in order to meet expenses and pay his people. Some mint growers were less fortunate.

The ladies were leading the group and managed to maintain a good speed despite their ongoing conversations and enjoying their lunches. The two girls, Mattie's friends, had become accustomed to their horses and saddles and were very relaxed as they all made their way back toward the ranch.

The three girls, riding side by side, continued to talk about Guatemala. The conversation drifted from one concern to another. Finally, Alicia looked at her two friends and shook her head.

"You know, we are just beating this whole situation to death. We need to quit talking about the 'what ifs' and concentrate on trusting the Lord to lead us in everything we do. Don't you both agree?"

Mattie looked at Bethany and then to Alicia, nodded her head, turned, and looked down the trail. The three maintained very little conversation for the remainder of the ride back to the ranch.

The horses sensed that they were almost home and nearing the ranch. They instantly picked up the pace, requiring the riders to rein them in. The riders began to relax as they neared the ranch.

The sun had dipped down behind the snow-capped peaks. At dusk, the riders viewed the ranch just ahead.

9

The group silently rode into the ranch and tied their horses to the rail fence surrounding the corral. Each of them, including Bethany and Alicia, removed their saddles and blankets and made their way to the tack room.

Everyone placed their saddles on the appropriate saddletree and headed back to their horses to remove their bridles and strap-on halters. Mattie's two friends were performing like old hands and didn't need to be told what to do around the horses.

Each one of them made their way to the big box containing all of the grooming brushes. Mattie showed her two friends how to use the currycomb and the brush. All of the horses were enjoying the special treatment as well as the bag of grain that they had over each of the horses' heads and snouts.

Dan was very quiet as he groomed his horse. He noticed how his faithful friend Sam was getting old and would soon be retired. Sam would be twenty on the 19th of May. He had ridden Sam since he was a three-year-old. Dan knew he would be sad when he would be forced to put his horse down. Oh, the adventures they had shared.

Dan walked to the rail and untied Sam's lead rope. Then he removed the halter and rubbed the proud horse's neck. Sam turned his head toward Dan and proceeded to nuzzle him under his left arm.

"OK, big guy; you head out to that sweet grass in the north pasture. I'll leave you alone for a few days. You need a good rest. You did a fine job with the herd these past few days. Only you and I know that you were the one setting an example for all those other Cayuses."

Sam was indeed the lead horse on the ranch. Each year, the ranch would buy one or two horses at a big auction near Pendleton. Dan had purchased Sam at that very same auction, now nearly eighteen years ago.

Sam had always assumed the position of leadership among the horses. Sometimes he would have to take several days of nips and an occasional kick to teach the new horses that he ate from the feed bin first. All of the horses seemed to know that he was in charge.

All three of the girls were talking softly to their horses as they groomed them. They quickly formed an attachment to the animals that served as their primary mode of transportation. The American quarter horse is unchallenged as the best breed for working cattle or trail riding. This breed of horse enjoys a very elite status among cattle ranchers.

The sun had completely disappeared behind the peaks to the west. Everyone except Garrett headed down the trail that leads from the corral to the ranch house. Garrett took a parallel trail that led to his cabin next to the small stream known as Little Three Creeks.

The mudroom adjoining the kitchen soon became pretty crowded. Boots were pulled off as coats and jackets were being hung on the big hooks along the wall.

Mildred walked in and greeted everyone. Mattie introduced her to Alicia and Bethany. Everyone had been in the saddle for hours and they were all weary.

Dan looked over the whole group and said, "You know, I have just come up with an idea. I think I'll take all of you out for a steak dinner at the Spur Café. I don't see any reason for anyone to have to cook tonight. Danny, give that dog of yours something to eat and then we can head for the restaurant. Mattie, I'd like you to go over to Garrett's cabin and tell him we're taking him out for a steak dinner. Mildred, grab your hat; you're coming with us."

"Mr. Branson, I don't wear no hat. You don't need to feed me, too."

"I *want* to feed you. I don't care if you don't have a hat. Do you have an appetite?"

Jessie commented, "You know, sweetheart, we all look pretty scuzzy to be going into a restaurant. If you want, the girls and I can all take showers and get pretty."

"You all look pretty enough for me. That sandwich you fed me earlier just didn't do the job to curb my appetite much longer."

"Dad, do you think they'll let us in, looking like we do?"

"Mattie, this isn't the five-star La Francias Restaurant in Chicago. This is Jake Sorenson's Café. He and Alice will welcome us with open arms."

Mattie walked back in the door and said that Garrett told her he was too tired to eat. "He wanted to know if you meant breakfast tomorrow." Everybody chuckled at Garrett's response.

"Okay then, let's get going. Come on everyone. The Suburban has enough seats for all of us."

Mildred walked up to Dan and whispered, "I need to go home right away, if it's okay with you. I haven't been home since the day before yesterday, and I need to feed my cat and my bird. I left them food, but I am worried that they didn't get enough to eat. Do you mind?"

"Wow, my crowd is beginning to thin out. I sure do understand. You go ahead, and we'll see you tomorrow. We do appreciate your taking care of Barney and holding down the fort while we were on the drive."

The six tired wranglers climbed into the Suburban and headed for the small local restaurant. Dan pulled into his normal parking spot behind the restaurant and then held open the front door to the restaurant as they filed in.

He pointed to the large table in the back and waved a hello to Alice, who he saw sitting at the counter. Being a Tuesday night, business was slow. Actually, no one was in the restaurant when they entered. Jake was leaning against the wall behind the counter, and Alice was perched on one of the stools.

"What's up, Bransons? Did your kitchen stove give out? We haven't seen any of you in a coon's age. Jess, did you and Mattie go on strike? Is that why we are getting the honor of your presence?"

"Actually, Alice, we just came in from driving the herd up into the mountains. We're all bushed, so Dan figured he would treat all of us to one of Jake's special steaks."

"I got just what you want," Jake yelled, "I got some great-looking steaks back here. Just tell Alice how you want them cooked, and let her know what kind of trimmings you would like."

Alice walked up to the table, set down water glasses for everyone, and then whipped out her order pad. She looked over the table and said, "Okay, who's first?"

Jessie looked up to Alice and said, "I'm going to have the fried chicken with mashed potatoes that you have listed as a special. The corn on the cob sounds good to me, too."

Mattie looked over to her two friends who were still studying the menu. "I'm going to have the fish and chips. That sounds really good to me. You two can have whatever sounds good to you. This is Dad's treat, so go for it."

Alicia looked at Bethany and said, "You know I was thinking about the fish and chips, too. What sounds good to you?"

"Actually, dear friend, I am going to go along with the guys. A steak sounds really good to me." She looked up at Alice and said, "I'd like a steak. I don't want it cooked like Mr. Branson will probably have his. I want mine cooked so it doesn't wiggle and doesn't have a chance at recovery. I love meat, but I don't eat it raw. I always believed that only wild animals ate meat that way."

"Alice, I want my steak rare," Dan said. "You tell old Jake that I mean rare. Tell him that if it looks like it might recover and walk out the door, it will be perfect. I'll still eat it. I'd also like a baked potato and some of that corn on the cob I see you got listed on your chalkboard. You can throw in a green salad with blue cheese, and I'll be about as happy as a man can get."

"You got it, Dan. Okay, little Dan, what are you having?"

"I'm going to have everything the same as Dad. But if it's still wiggling, I won't eat it."

They all gave Alice their beverage orders and went back to their conversations. Alice turned from the table, took about three steps, and literally yelled to Jake, "I need three hunks of bovine. One still walking, one hurt badly, and one ready for burial. I need a buzzard with soft spuds and a couple of deep water floaters with fries."

. Jake stuck his head through opening behind the counter, grinned, and said, "You got it."

Alice had been working at the Spur for nearly twenty years. She took a job working for Jake when she got out of high school. She was not only a fixture in the restaurant, but also one of the most colorful characters in town.

Everyone's meal came just as they had ordered. Close to seven o'clock now, the sun had long since disappeared behind the skyline to the west. They were all eating quietly when a huge motor home pulled in beside the restaurant. Dan could tell by looking at it that it was one of those fancy rigs that could cost up to a half-million dollars.

As the two people from the motor home entered the restaurant, everyone noticed that they were dressed for a much fancier facility. The man, wearing a dark suit, appeared to be in his late forties. The woman, dressed in a sleek, tailored pants suit, wearing six-inch high heels, was probably about the same age, but dressed and acted like she was in her twenties.

They took a booth close to where the Bransons were sitting and began to study the menu. The lady seemed to be very displeased with the options listed on it and made her disapproval known to her male friend. The Branson party couldn't tell if they were married, as he wore no wedding ring, yet she had rings on virtually every finger.

"My dear, do you have *comfit du canard?*" the woman asked Alice in an aloof tone and with a conceited look on her face. "Or have I said or asked for something you don't understand?"

"Madame, si vous voulez confiance du Canard, alors vous aurez à régler pour notre spécial qui est le poulet frit avec des pommes de terre écrasées, servie avec des épis de maïs."

Alice rattled off her reply in impeccable French. She even had the proper accent.

The totally stunned lady looked at Alice and said, "I'm sorry, I didn't understand your answer."

"Lady, my answer was in French. You ordered in French. You asked for a duck cooked, consistent with French cuisine. I said if you want something like that, you're in the wrong town. I said we have fried chicken with mashed potatoes, served with corn on the cob. It's on special today."

"Seth, let's go somewhere else."

The man looked at Alice, winked, and said, "Give us two hamburgers. We don't want any pickles, but we would like lots of lettuce."

Alice nodded, turned, and yelled at Jake: "Two gut bombs scratch the sour cucumbers. Add extra leaves."

Alice brought her water pitcher to the Bransons' table, winked, and said, "Four years of French in high school. I love the language. I always thought I might go there someday and wanted to know the language. That's the first time I have had a chance to use it in years."

The Bransons' and their guests were still sitting at their table when the strange couple finished their hamburgers, paid their bill, and left.

"Wow!" Alice exclaimed. "I'm going to have to do that more often. That guy left me a twelve-dollar tip for an eight-dollar bill."

"Alice, you really were fantastic. I believe that guy, Seth, I think his lady friend said his name was, thought so too. I don't think they're married, and I would bet that they won't ever get married. I think the guy was mortified at the lady's statement," Dan commented.

He looked at his watch and noted that it was nearly eight in the evening. He looked around the big table and noted that everyone seemed to have eaten as much of their dinner as they wanted.

"Well, gang, I think we're all done and ought to head back to the ranch. My sleep sort of got split up last night. I could use a good night's rest."

Dan picked up the bill that Alice had placed next to his plate. He walked up to the register and paid and then walked back over to the table and deposited an appropriate tip.

10

Dan looked up into the sky and noted that it was already late in the morning. He was on his way to the corral to check on the horses when he discovered Danny already there, putting a horse bridle on Nugget, his horse.

"What's up son? Where are you heading?"

"I already fed the stock and gave them a little grain. I thought I would go out to the big hay barn near the road and see about all those cats. I figured I would see if we had any more kittens. I think the count is way over a hundred now."

"Are you going to put a saddle on him?"

"No, I like riding him bareback unless I am going to spend a lot of time riding," Danny said as he jumped up on Nugget's back.

"Do you want company?"

"Sure, Dad, I always like riding with you. Sam isn't here in the corral. I think he is out by the irrigation pond. Do you want me to get him for you?"

"That's okay. This should work."

Dan put his fingers between his teeth and made a loud shrill whistle that was almost painful to the ears. Sam, who had his head down munching grass, instantly lifted his head and looked towards the corral. The big horse began to trot and then broke out in a dead run toward the source of the whistle, knowing it to be his master, Dan Branson.

"I sure wish I could get Nugget to come to me like that. I always have to go up and grab him to get him to the hitching rail. Dad, how did you teach Sam to respond like that? Did you use some sort of a trick or did he just learn that by himself?"

When Sam arrived at the corral, puffing hard after the run, he walked up to Dan and just stood there. Dan had retrieved his bridle while Sam was on his way to the corral. He slipped on the bridle and swung himself up on the big horse's back.

Danny was sitting patiently on Nugget's back.

"Actually, I didn't have to teach him. When he was a three-year-old he would start to wander away whenever I came up to him. I would let out one of my whistles and just stand there. He would stop, turn, and look at me. Then, he would trot back to me. That's how we first became acquainted. Now he knows that when I whistle, he is supposed to come to me."

"That's neat. I still wish I could teach that to Nugget. Sam is getting pretty old, isn't he? How much longer do you think he will last?"

"That's a tough question. He is my friend, and his loss is going to be tough on me. However, I know that day is coming. Some horses live to their late twenties. I believe Sam has a good chance of living another couple of years. He will be twenty in June."

Dan and Danny were riding along the fence bordering the east side of the ranch. They were looking out into the fields, seeing the wheeled waterlines actively shooting large streams of water onto the thirsty alfalfa. They were headed for the hay barn located near the north end of the main ranch.

"Danny, when you were about eight years old, We knelt beside your bed one night, and you asked Jesus to come into your heart and direct your life. I believe that you did truly give your life to Him. How do you feel about the way things are happening now in our family?"

"You know, Dad, I've been thinking a lot about that lately. I think about how God has led you to serve him. I was really scared when you went to South America. I thought maybe you wouldn't come back. When I heard you tell us about everything that happened down there, I got even more scared. Do you think the Lord will look after Mattie the way he watched over you?"

"I believe that without a doubt. Once you belong to Him, He wants you to put Him in charge. Some people like to run things themselves, but they usually find out later that God always had a better plan. I don't think those girls are going to have a picnic in Guatemala, but I think the Lord will be watching over them. Sometimes He lets you go through some pretty heavy stuff in order for Him to fulfill His plan."

They stopped their horses just outside the open-ended barn and looked in. Only about fifty bales of alfalfa were left in the barn since the winter feeding of the stock had pretty much depleted the contents.

They dismounted and walked into the hay barn. They heard meows coming from the backside of the small stack of hay. The two squeezed themselves between the bales and saw a large yellow cat lying on her side with five tiny kittens nursing. They looked around and discovered another cat, this one gray, with a similar-sized litter. Dan noticed that cats were everywhere.

The two walked back to their horses, mounted, and continued their ride around the perimeter of the ranch. As the main ranch was exactly two square miles, they made the decision to cut across at one of the cross fences and head back to the corral.

"Danny, what you just saw is how God's plan is working here on this earth. He brings new life into the world and he takes life out. Just like in Sam's case, he did his job well, and the time has come for him to enjoy a little leisure time. Ultimately, the time will come for him to die, just like it will be for you and me someday. Not soon we hope, but the time will come.

"We don't know when God will say 'Enough' and let the people of earth go into self-destruction. It will happen because our Bible tells us it will. That's why the Bible also tells us to be prepared. I honestly believe that the girls have been called by the Lord to go to Guatemala. While they are gone, we have to accept whatever takes place or whatever happens to any or all of them as being part of His plan."

They jumped off their horses and removed their bridles. Dan asked Danny to get a couple of grain bags for Sam and Nugget. A few minutes later, they walked slowly back to the ranch house. Danny was staring intently at the ground when he stopped, turned to his dad, and said, "Thanks, Dad. I love talking with you, just the two of us. You really do inspire me."

Danny moved to his dad, stopped, and put his arms around him. They stood there hugging each other for a full minute.

"Hey, you two," Jessie said. "Where have you been? We saw you guys ride past the house going north. We didn't see you ride back. What have you two been up to?"

"Mom, we got a couple more litters of kittens in the north hay barn. Dad and I have been talking about life and death. He says that if the Lord wants Mattie and her friends in Guatemala, then God will look after them. We're supposed to trust God and His plan."

"Sounds like you two have been having pretty heavy conversations." She walked over to Danny and gave him a hug.

"Dan, what time are you planning to fly the girls back to Portland? They say they are packed and ready to go whenever you are. Are we all going, or are you going to fly them alone?"

"Actually, I was thinking that we could all fly over. If we left the ranch at about eleven, we would be in Portland around twelve-thirty. That being the case, I thought we might run up the hill to Rose's Delicatessen and have lunch. I don't believe any of you have been there. They make quite a sandwich. What do you think?"

"How soon do you want to leave?"

"Let me know as soon as everyone is ready to get into the Suburban. I'll call the Redmond Airport now and ask them to drag our bird out of the hangar."

Jessie walked over to the doorway and shouted, "Girls, grab your stuff. We're all going to fly to Portland. Danny, you need to come along, too."

Dan made the call to the airport and asked them to pull his airplane out of the hangar. They advised him that it would be on the ramp by the time he arrived.

The drive to the Redmond Airport takes about twenty minutes depending on the traffic. Being a Wednesday they wouldn't have a lot of weekend sightseers on the road, making the trip even faster. Upon arrival, they parked the Suburban behind the flight-line office and walked over to Dan's 310 Cessna.

"She's all ready to go, Mr. Branson. I cleaned the windows as we had a dust storm over the weekend, and a lot of dust accumulated."

"Thanks Neal. I appreciate your fast action. We're going over to Portland, and we'll be back before dark. When we get back, I'll park the plane by the gas truck if you're not here. You can top off the tips with 100-octane. Don't worry about anything else, as I will check her out pretty thoroughly myself. By the way, welcome back. This is your second year here, isn't it?"

"Yes sir. I sure do like being here. I am having a great time, and I'm looking forward to the summer when we get all of the fly-in tourists."

"Okay gang, you can all climb in while I check to see if our bird is ready to fly."

The flight into Portland was smooth. They didn't encounter any bumps. Dan said the flight was like flying down a greased wire. He taxied his plane to the Flightcraft transit area and walked into the flight-line office, coming back out with a set of keys for a Toyota sedan. Danny loaded the girls' luggage into the trunk of the rental car.

"Dad, this is not the way to Multnomah. Where are we going?"

"I thought I would show you all a great place to have lunch. You're hungry, aren't you? We have lots of time. School doesn't start again until tomorrow."

11

Everyone was quiet as Dan exited the Banfield Freeway, crossed over the Willamette River, and then headed up Burnside. He turned right partway up the hill and stopped across the street from a restaurant that displayed a sign that read Rose's Delicatessen. He had a big smile on his face when he motioned for everyone to get out and follow him.

As they walked into the restaurant, they were led along an area displaying glass cases that had not large —but *huge* — cakes and donuts.

They were seated, and the waitress handed out menus to everyone. Dan looked around the table and said, "Don't any of you be bashful. This is my treat. Order whatever strikes your fancy."

Danny looked up from his menu and asked, "Is it okay for me to order an LS Supreme sandwich? It's pretty expensive."

"I said you could order whatever strikes your fancy. That means you can order *whatever* you like."

The girls all looked at each other and decided on different sandwiches. Jessie looked at Dan and suggested that they split a sandwich. Dan winked and told her that was a good idea. The waitress took their order and brought their drinks. In a few minutes, she brought a large tray to the table and began placing plates in front of everyone.

"You've got to be kidding," Mattie said with a loud voice. "I don't think all three of us could eat this one sandwich. It's huge! It must weigh at least two pounds!"

"Look at mine. It's grinning at me." Danny was holding his sandwich between his hands, and it was sagging severely, looking like a giant mouth.

"Mr. Branson, if Bethany and I each gain 10 pounds as a result of these past few days, you are to blame. Neither of us has had the chance to run at all. We usually run two or three miles every day. I think we had better do five miles each day for the rest of the week. Maybe we can burn off these sandwiches."

"Hey Dad, this is good. I don't care if I bust a gut; I'm going to down this whole sandwich. I can't believe they can make them this big. How about you, Sis? How are you doing on your giant sandwich?"

"Danny, I'm not like you. I can't eat this whole sandwich in one sitting. I'm going to take this back to the dorm and hide it. I think I can munch on this for a couple of days."

"I'm glad that your dad and I made the decision to split a sandwich. I am sure he knew in advance what we would all be facing when we got our orders. Mattie, I know you are thinking of hiding the rest of your sandwich for later, but remember it has mayo in it and will go bad pretty fast. Eat what you can now and forget about the rest."

Dan confessed, "I have been here before. About a year ago when I was trading the Bonanza for the 310, the salesman brought me here for lunch. I made the same mistake that all of you made. I couldn't finish the sandwich and even then I had a stomachache for the rest of the day. However, I do agree that the food is great and very tasty. Anyone want dessert?"

The women all let out groans. Danny, on the other hand, had that look on his face that indicated that he wanted to try one of the desserts displayed in the glass cases near the entrance.

"You've got to be kidding, little brother. You are going to burst if you eat anything more. I can't believe it, but you managed to eat your whole sandwich. Where did you put it?"

"Danny, I'm your mom. I think you have had enough. I don't want to hear you moaning and groaning all night when we get home. I don't care what they say about teenage boys. You are going to stop eating now."

Dan was staring at the ceiling. He had no intention of interfering between his wife and his son. He made the decision that getting involved would not be in his best interest. He motioned for the waitress and asked for the bill. Almost in unison, they all declined her offer to provide dessert menus. She had a giant, knowing smile on her face as she encountered this type of over-indulgence every day.

Dan paid the bill and then held the door for everyone as they exited the restaurant and made their way back across the street to their rental car.

Dan took the most direct route back to Multnomah, taking the Banfield freeway to 82nd Avenue and then just a short distance to the campus.

They pulled into a parking space not far from the women's dormitory. Everyone got out of the car and assembled near the trunk. Alicia and Bethany didn't have much luggage as they had only brought overnight bags.

"Mr. and Mrs. Branson, I know that I am speaking for both Bethany and myself," Alicia said. "I want you two to know how much we appreciate all you have done for us. The cattle drive was an experience that neither of us will soon forget. Your home is spectacular! You truly were right when you said that the Lord has blessed your family abundantly.

"I was blessed beyond belief when we came face to face with Angelo. When he told me that he knew my parents, I was literally blown away. I have gone many years wondering if they were with God. When he said that they were proud of me, my faith was bolstered as well as my trust in God."

"Mr. Branson, you two have been more than kind to both of us," Bethany said. "As a result of how kind you both have been, we now both consider ourselves part of your family. I'm like Alicia. My dad died when I was just a little girl. Now I know that he not only loved me very much, but that he is watching over me from up above. Words can't express what these past few days have done to my life. My faith has never been stronger."

"Mom and Dad, I love you a bunch. Little brother, you, too, are very special to me. Thank you all for giving my friends and me a weekend we will never forget. By the way, Dad, you should know that all three of us have decided to skip dinner tonight."

Following lots of hugs and a few tears from both Bethany and Alicia, Dan, Jessie, and Danny climbed back into their rental car and headed back to the airport.

Dan looked at his watch and noted the time was just a few minutes after four in the afternoon. He calculated that they would be back at the ranch by six.

12

"State Department Operator, what number do you wish, please?"

"Hello, this Dan Branson. I am calling from Oregon, and I'm trying to locate an Ed Harris. I believe he is a military attaché to the Argentine Embassy. Can you help me?"

"Let me transfer you to the Capital Information Operator. Perhaps she can locate the man you are looking for."

Dan leaned back in the chair behind his desk. His office was located at the end of the hall on the east side of the ranch house. He spent several hours every month in his private space, keeping the records for their ranch. In less than a minute, he heard a new voice on the phone.

"This is Hope. I am the Capital Operator. I understand that you are trying to locate Ed Harris. Is that correct?"

"Yes, that's correct. I knew him through the Argentine Embassy. Can you help me locate him?"

"Yes, Mr. Harris is now with the Central Intelligence Agency. Would you like me to connect you with his office?"

"Please do."

"Mr. Harris' office, this is Pennie Randolph. How can I help you?"

"My name is Dan Branson. I'm a former acquaintance of Ed's. I was with him for a couple of days in Argentina. Is he available to speak with me?"

"Just a moment. I'll see if he is available."

"Hey cowboy, is that you on the other end of the line? Are you the same guy that took on the Scagleone Cartel a few years ago?"

"Hi Ed. Yes, that sure enough was me. I hate to bother you, but I have a few questions. Perhaps you can provide me with the answers. Have you got a minute to talk?"

"You bet. Shoot."

"Ed, I believe you know about my commitment to the Lord. I realize we haven't spoken in six years, but things are happening in my family into which perhaps you can give me some insight.

"My daughter, Mattie, is now nineteen. She has been attending a Bible college in Portland, Oregon. She and two of her friends have been called by the Lord to assist a lady who runs a women's refuge and an orphanage in Guatemala. They plan to be there for two months. I have been doing a little checking, and from what I can tell, they are going to be visiting a pretty troubled area. Am I right?"

"Wow, Dan, you don't know the half of it. President Otto Pérez Molina has his hands full. Guatemala has more crime and problems than any other country I know of. I have to tell you that our government is maintaining a hands-off policy. We keep clear of everything that is going on. Can you talk your kid into doing her mission work somewhere else in the world?"

"Not a chance. She is committed to going. They will probably be down there by mid-June and won't be due to come home until mid-August. I understand you are now with the CIA. Is that a step up for you? Are you one of our covert spies now?"

"That's not really funny, Dan. I do a lot of things for our Uncle, but covert ops are not one of them. I can give you the names of our contacts in Guatemala City, but beyond that, you will be on your own."

"I didn't mean to offend you, Ed. I was just making conversation along with trying to figure out where you are on the food chain. I would sincerely like to chat with your guys down there, if that is permissible."

"Normally that would be out of the question. We are a very low profile organization. My guys do not work through our consulate. They are pretty much on their own. I would need to talk to the boss and see how he feels about giving you some highly classified information. I can't do that over the phone until I have a secure line. Give me your number, and I'll try to get back to you within twenty-four hours. Don't be offended if I can't pull it off. I promise you that I will try, though."

"Thank you, Ed. I didn't know of anyone else in Washington. I tried to get through to our senator, but he has not returned my calls."

"Dan, I have a lot better connection than any of your senators. Trust me, if anyone can get you a contact in Guatemala, I can do it. The politicians don't have the right contacts, but I do. Don't bother to contact the consulate as they have their hands pretty much tied by the higher-ups.

"By the way, did you hear about Carmelita Hernandez, the Argentine ambassador's wife?"

"I have to tell you, we corresponded for a couple of years, and then we sort of lost contact with each other. What about Carmelita?" Dan asked.

85

"I'm sorry to tell you that she died two years ago of cancer. Miguel is no longer the ambassador. He hasn't been for nearly four years. I understand that he is working with a Christian missionary somewhere in Bolivia. You must have had some influence on the Hernandezes. As I heard the story, they abandoned everything in Buenos Aires, turned everything over to their son, and the two of them went out to become evangelical missionaries."

"Thanks for filling me in on that, Ed. I am truly saddened that I did not keep in touch with the Hernandezes. Carmelita was a fine woman, and I admired her and her husband very much. I'll wait to hear from you in the next couple of days."

"You got it. Wait for my call."

Jessie walked into Dan's office and sat down in the chair facing him as he sat at his desk. She saw Dan with his head in his hands, looking down at the top of the desk.

"What's going on sweetheart? You look distressed. Did you hear something bad about the kids' chances in Guatemala? Do you have something you need to tell me?"

"Ed Harris, the guy with the State Department that I met on the plane to Buenos Aires is now with the CIA. He is going to try and get me a source to communicate with in Guatemala.

"The reason I am distressed is that he just told me that Carmelita Hernandez, the Argentine ambassador's wife, died two years ago of cancer. Miguel is no longer ambassador. Actually he and his wife became evangelical Christians. Ed told me that he believes Miguel is working with a missionary somewhere in Bolivia."

"I am sad to hear that, Dan. I know you spoke to them about the Lord and that you really cared for both of them. If I remember right, you were guests in their home, and he also helped you with transportation back to us. I believe that we should put Miguel on our prayer list. I am sure that he needs all the help that can be given if he is working with a missionary in South America."

Dan and Jessie walked into the living room and took their usual seats facing the fireplace. Although a fire was not burning, they both sat staring into the pile of ashes that accumulated from previous fires. They spent a long time just sitting together.

Finally, Dan spoke. He cleared his throat, looked at the big Remington bronze sitting on the coffee table, and then he looked at Jessie.

"I don't know why, but I think we ought to either find a different place for that big thing or sell it. We both know that it has to be worth a small fortune."

"Do we need the money? I never thought about our selling any of the art that we inherited with this house. I'll try to figure out another place to put it. What gave you this idea about the bronze?"

"Actually, I don't know where that statement came from. It does kind of block some of our view of the fire when it's going. Perhaps we should not become too attached to all of the material things that the Lord has put into our lives."

* * *

At five o'clock the next morning, the phone rang, waking both Dan and Jessie. Dan leaned over and quickly grabbed the phone, assuming it was some sort of emergency call. What else could it be this early?

"Howdy, cowboy. Did I wake you? We are all at work here in DC. I figured that you have been up for at least an hour, out milking cows or whatever you do early in the morning."

"You're both right and wrong, Ed. You were right about waking me up. You were wrong about my getting up and milking cows. This is a cattle ranch, not a dairy. I generally roll out of the sack at six. Right now it's only five here in Oregon."

"Sorry about that, old friend. I wanted to get to you and let you know that you will be getting a call from one of my associates. I can't give you a name because this is not a secure line. I don't know when you will hear from him; I just know that you will get a call within the next few days.

"As you probably already know, we have information on just about everybody. You apparently threw a big monkey wrench into the operations of one of the world's biggest crime families.

"I'm talking about the Scagleone family in Italy. Apparently, you really rattled their cage. From what I have been able to find out, they don't want to come near you. You and one of your associates, whoever that was, made such an impression with the top guy that he put out an order to stay clear of you. You have my respect. The people here think you must be some sort of miracle worker with a guardian angel."

Dan had a broad smile on his face when he said, "Thanks for the call, Ed. I'll look forward to hearing from your guys. I still have thirty minutes. Can I go back to sleep now?"

13

Dan hung up the phone and rolled over on his side facing Jessie, still smiling. She was staring into his eyes, searching for some clue as to what he was thinking.

"The people at the CIA seem to think I have some kind of a guardian angel looking after me. They say that the people who were harassing the Manderas in Argentina were one of the worst crime families in the world.

"Ed said that the person you and I know as Michael put a scare into the head guy, some big wig named Scagleone. This big shot made a mandate that no one was to bother us. They're scared of us."

"God does work in mysterious ways, doesn't he? Did he say anything about having a contact for the girls in Guatemala?"

"He said someone would be contacting us within a day or two. Apparently, the CIA has operatives down there. Honestly, I am not surprised. I think those guys have operatives everywhere. Maybe they're listening to us right now."

"I hope you're kidding. The way things are going on around the world is pretty scary. That war that you were in is still going on. When will it all end? When will the world recognize that God wants everyone to love one another, not kill one another?"

"Unfortunately, our Bible says that the world will never surrender to God until after Jesus returns. The leaders of the world keep talking about a war to end all wars, but that will never happen."

"I seem to have talked right through my chance to get another thirty minutes of sleep. The clock says six. I'm going to jump into the shower, and then I'll head down to the corral and feed the horses."

Dan slowly walked over to the big window facing the fields with the peaks of the Cascades in the background. His eye caught some movement below. He glanced down to the yard and saw Danny walking out toward the corral.

"Looks like our number one son got up early. He is on his way out to the corral. I sense that he has some deep concerns about his sister and her friends going to Guatemala. I tried to put him at ease, but I think he has to work this entire thing out in his own mind. I am sure that he will finally come to the conclusion that he needs to put all of his fears and concerns on God's altar."

"Now, I am going to take a longer shower than I originally planned since I have extra time. Do you want to go down to the Spur Café for breakfast?"

"No, I think I will make waffles. Danny loves waffles, and I haven't made them for a while. I'm going to go down to the kitchen and get started. You take your shower, and I'll get breakfast going. Don't take too long. The waffles will get cold."

When Dan had finished showering, he dressed and headed down the stairs to the kitchen. He entered the kitchen, walked behind his wife working at the sink, lifted the back of her hair and kissed her on the neck.

"Hey, Cowboy, you're getting kind of frisky for this early in the morning. Take a seat over there by your son. He has already consumed three big waffles. I'll have another one coming out in just a minute. Do you want a couple of eggs to go on top of your waffles?"

"The eggs sound great. You know I love eggs. I like them any way you want to cook them. If you can do them sunny side up, that would be perfect.

"Hi Danny. You got up kind of early. I saw you heading out to the corral. Are all of the horses okay this morning?"

"They all look great. I didn't give them any grain. I figured maybe I would give them each a snootful tonight."

Jessie poured herself a mug of coffee and walked into the breakfast area, carrying Dan's breakfast consisting of two eggs on top of his waffle and two pieces of bacon. She sat down on the bench with her back to the window and faced her two guys.

She was wearing a chenille robe with big yellow flowers embroidered on the front and back. She had the robe wrapped tightly around her body with the collar turned up in back.

"I think I'll just have coffee. I have been eating too much lately. Guys don't seem to gain weight as fast as women do. You guys can gain five pounds and then shed it just like it was water. Women can't do that."

"Since when have you started worrying about your weight? You are perfect. I don't believe you have an ounce of fat anywhere on you that doesn't belong. You have no reason to be worrying about gaining weight."

"Can't you two talk about something else? I am trying to see how many of Mom's waffles I can eat at one sitting. I am starting on number four. I can see that Mom has one more in the waffle iron. Dad, do I get that one, or do you want another?"

"You go for it, son. I don't plan to set any new waffle-eating records. I can't compete with you."

Dan had finished his breakfast and was studying the skyline visible through the eight-foot-wide window in the kitchen eating area. His elbows were resting on the table while he held his coffee mug with both hands. The sound of the telephone ringing grabbed his attention.

"Do you want me to get it?" Danny asked.

"No, it's probably for me.

"Hello, this is Dan Branson."

"Dan, my name is Randy Johnson. Ed Harris asked me to give you a call."

"Hi, Randy, give me a minute. I want to take this call in my office. Please hang on."

"Danny, please hang this up when you hear me pick it up in my office." Dan headed quickly to his office, sat down, and picked up the phone.

"Go ahead, Randy. Ed Harris told me someone would be calling me."

"Well, Dan, Ed has told me quite a bit about you. You and I have never met, but I have to be truthful and tell you that I heard the stories about some crazy cowboy raising a ruckus with the heavyweight mafia guys down in Argentina. My hat goes off to you, cowboy."

"Thanks for the compliment, Randy. I am glad you called. Are you in Guatemala now?"

"Actually, I am in Belize. Blake Donavan, Grant Adams, and I are working with some exporters down here. I will be back in Guatemala City by the end of the week. We are the total complement of people working for the company, just the three of us. Blake and Grant will probably stay here on Ambergris Island for another week or two.

"Harris says you have a daughter coming down to Guatemala for a couple of months. I would really recommend that you ask her to change her destination. This place is really a mess right now. The crime families are fighting among themselves. The Colombians seem to be the strongest. I don't see things getting better any time soon."

"I understand your concern. Unfortunately, Mattie, my daughter, is a very strong and stubborn young lady. She and her friends have committed themselves to helping a lady that is running a small orphanage and a women's refuge near Guatemala City."

"If your daughter is planning to work with a lady named Charlene Pearson, her place is about 50 kilometers south of Guatemala City, towards Antigua. Is that the person?"

"Yes, that is her name. I don't know her location. I am surprised that you know about her."

"The reason I know about her is that her place is located right in the middle of the worst area in all of Guatemala. Your kid couldn't have picked a worse place to go. Charlene is a fine woman. She does a great service to the area, but she has had her problems.

"The only reason I know anything at all about her is that one of her teenage orphan boys ran off about a year ago, came into Guatemala City, and stole a car...my car. They caught the kid, sent him back to Charlene, and I got my car back, although it looked like it had been in a demolition derby."

"What a small world. The reason I asked for Ed Harris' help was that I might need to have a contact in

Guatemala in case one of the girls has some sort of problem. Could they possibly get a hold of you, if that becomes the case? I really should ask if this is something that you would be willing to do."

"No problem, Dan. My partners and I are actually sort of in the agriculture business down here. We really do run a consulting business. If the girls have any problems at all, they are certainly free to give me a call. Give me your email address. I don't like to give out too much information over the phone."

"You bet. Have you got a pencil handy?"

"Ready to copy."

"Our email address is branson@triplepeaks.com."

"Got it, Dan. I'll send my cell phone number to your email. Please let your girls know that we are available, day or night, if they need help."

"Thanks a million, Randy. I feel much better now. Just knowing that they have someone who is closer than three thousand miles is a great relief."

14

"Was that our contact in Guatemala?"

"Yes, it was, Jessie. Three guys are down there. They are in the agriculture consulting business. The one guy by the name of Randy Johnson, the man I just talked to, has partners who are named Blake Donavan, and Grant Adams, who are currently in Belize. However, Randy will be in Guatemala City by the end of the week. Jessie, this guy knows Charlene Pearson. At least we have a contact now if we need one."

"Are they CIA operatives? Do we know anything about them?"

"All we know is that Ed Harris referred them to us. I think we have to put some trust in that. I doubt that he would have referred them to us unless he had a high degree of confidence in these three men."

"Sounds like things are coming together. I am feeling better all of the time. I wonder how the girls in Portland are doing. I imagine they have been packed and ready to go from the minute they got back from the cattle drive.

"I'm going to go take my shower. Where will you be when I come down?"

"I have some work to do in the office. I will probably still be crunching numbers. I hope to get an idea about what the buyers will be paying for peppermint oil. As you know, we kept our oil from last year. The prices they were offering would have only brought us to the break-even point. I think we're going to do better this year. They know we have fourteen barrels out in the round barn. I think they want it."

"Okay, see you when I am beautiful again."

Dan watched Jessie leave the kitchen and then heard her climbing the stairs leading to the second floor and their bedroom. Less than a minute later, he heard the shower running. He knew that he was the luckiest man on the face of the earth. Jessie truly was a beautiful woman, and the love between them ran very deep. They never questioned that God Himself put the two together.

* * *

The phone rang on Dan's desk, taking him away from the numbers he had been juggling for the past few minutes.

"Hello, this is Dan Branson."

"Hi Dad, it's me. I just wanted you to know that we have got our schedules worked out. We're all going to be flying on American Airlines. We leave Portland on the 15th of June, and we fly back on the 17th of August. We leave at 6:30 in the morning, and we land in Guatemala City at 8:30 that same night. We have about a five-hour layover in Dallas, Texas. You were right on with your estimate of the mileage. It is right at 3,000 miles from home to Guatemala.

"Like I told you, the school takes care of all of our reservations. I have to pay for my ticket, which comes to a little over $800. As you already know, Mr. Guest and Mr. Skaggs will pay all of Bethany's expenses, but Alicia is pretty worried about the money, as her mom is on a pretty tight budget."

"Mattie, you know that your mother and I have some bucks tucked away that are committed to the Lord's work. Please tell Alicia that we will come up with her expenses. Would you do that for me?"

"Why don't you tell her yourself, Dad? She's sitting right next to me."

"Hello, Mr. Branson. Mattie said you wanted to talk to me. What can I do for you?"

"The question is not what you can do for me, but what we can do for you. I just told Mattie that her mother and I always keep some of God's money on hand for whenever we need to put it to work. I believe your expenses are something that fits right into that category and our fund."

"I am sure that the Lord would like us to help out with your expenses. Please tell whoever is in charge of making all of your reservations that we will be paying for your tickets or, for that matter, anything else that requires money."

"Thank you so much, Mr. Branson! My mom will be *so* relieved. When I told her how much the trip was going to cost, she said she would have to see if she could borrow the money. This will make her very happy. She really wants me to go on this trip to Guatemala. I think she would be willing to sacrifice just about anything to make it possible for me to go. Here's Mattie again."

"Hey, Dad, you're the greatest! You don't know how lucky I feel being your daughter. Is Mom there? I would really like to talk to her."

"She's upstairs taking a shower. I think she is trying to run the well dry because she been in there now for about a half-hour. I can still hear the water running. Do you want me to have her call you as soon as she comes down? I don't know long that will be. I know she loves when you call."

"No, I have to go to class in about five minutes. Tell her I will give her a call after dinner. Do you have any idea how much I love you two?"

"Yes, baby, we know. We love you a big bunch, too. I'll tell Mom to expect your call this evening."

* * *

Around seven in the evening, the phone rang. Dan looked at Jessie still sitting at the dinner table and nodded towards the phone on the wall.

"I'm sure that's probably for you, baby. Why don't you head for your big chair in the living room, and I'll tell her you will be right there."

"Hello, this is Dan Branson."

"Hi Dad, it's me."

"Hang on, baby, your mom is going into the living room. She'll pick up the …. there she is. Go for it ladies."

The two women talked for nearly an hour. They would have a quiet conversation often followed by a loud laugh. Occasionally, Dan would hear a light chuckle. Mother-daughter sessions could last for hours. Dan often said that the Bransons were fortunate that they have one of those telephone plans that do not charge for long distance calls.

Dan enlisted Danny's help in doing the dinner dishes. Dinner had been macaroni and cheese served with orange slices and boiled, fresh spinach. Jessie always placed a giant hunk of butter on top of the spinach when she served it. This was one of the family favorites.

***

June 15 came around a lot faster than anyone in the Branson family could have anticipated. The big calendar hanging on the wall next to the mudroom door had the countdown dates crossed off. Jessie crossed off the 14th and instantly had a lump in her throat. Dan, sensing her turmoil, walked to stand beside her and put his arms around her.

"I figure we should leave here about three this afternoon. I want to take the girls out to dinner tonight. Nothing fancy— just a quiet dinner. Maybe we can all eat at the hotel near the airport. I made reservations for the three of us to stay there tonight. Mattie has her car so she can drive her friends to the hotel. Is all of this okay with you?"

"Sounds like a great idea. If the girls are to catch a 6:30 flight, then I assume we should all be over to the airport at 5:30. What do you think?"

"I agree. Mattie said that the school wanted to bring the girls and their luggage to the airport. I offered to provide them with transportation, but she said they had made it clear that the school wanted to do it."

* * *

Time was going by very fast for Dan and Jessie. When the girls showed up for dinner, they ate quickly as the girls were too keyed up to get involved in any heavy conversations. When they finished their dinner and dessert, Mattie suggested that they get back to their dorm and finish packing. Jessie seemed surprised that they weren't totally packed. Mattie said that she had packed and unpacked at least a dozen times, trying to make sure she hadn't forgotten anything. Alicia and Bethany confirmed that they too had been going through the very same drill.

Dan and Jessie were both restless through the night. Dan lay awake until past midnight. Several times he heard Danny in the next bed, tossing and turning. Jessie was doing the same.

Dan looked over at the bedside clock and noted the time to be 5 am. He leaned over, turned on the lamp beside the bed, and got up. A few seconds later, Jessie got up and headed for the bathroom. Dan turned to wake up Danny and saw him sitting up in bed. He climbed out of bed and started to put his clothes back on. In record time, Jessie vacated the bathroom and turned it over to her two guys.

They took the hotel shuttle to the terminal and arrived just a few minutes before 5:30. When they walked into the terminal, they saw the girls, Mr. Guest, and Mr. Skaggs all standing by the TSA entrance, waiting for them to arrive. They were early, as only a few people were in line for the security check.

The Bransons introduced their son to the two gentlemen and then all eight engaged in trivial chatter. Dan looked at Jessie and could see her begin to tense.

She was holding back a flood of tears. When she hugged Mattie tightly, the tears began to flow down both of their cheeks. Next was Dan's turn and then her brother, Danny. The girls also had plenty of hugs for the two gentlemen.

The Bransons went outside to wait and watch for the big plane to take off. Even though the girls would never see, they all waved silently.

15

The top floor of the Hernandez Building was elegantly furnished. The entire floor was occupied by one company: Consolidated International Trading Corporation. The elevator reached the fourteenth floor and would operate only after placing an electronically encoded access card in the proper slot.

The elevator opened to a large carpeted reception area that was better than twice as large in comparison to most office reception areas. The only thing anyone could observe as they exited the elevator was a large desk with a strikingly beautiful, dark-haired girl named Rosalina sitting behind it. She appeared to be in her late twenties and was unquestionably selected for her poise and beauty. She had a large clipboard beside her computer that indicated which visitors were expected and when they might arrive.

Behind the wall that encompassed the reception area were sixteen desks. Six of the desks were occupied by men and women busily working the keyboards of computers. The rest of the desks were empty and unused. Beyond the sixteen desks were two very large doors centered in an elegantly paneled wall. The doors opened into a single office.

The office itself was gigantic. It had floor-to-ceiling plate glass windows on three sides, indicating that it took up literally half of the top floor of the building. The open deck that encompassed the office extended out ten feet to a three-foot wall. The spectacular view displayed all of Guatemala City and the surrounding areas.

The inside furnishings were elegant in design and were dispersed into two sitting areas. No chair was directly in front of the huge desk, indicating that whoever was visiting the man behind the desk would more than likely be standing. Every person employed by the company spoke both Castilian Spanish as well as Portuguese. Only a few spoke English.

The heavyset man behind the desk, Hernando Banderas, was sucking on a huge Cuban cigar. He knew he was fat as he currently weighed in at nearly 300 pounds. He loved food and made no effort to exercise. He spent his entire time sitting behind his giant desk.

He pushed aside some papers as he glared at the short, thin man standing before him.

"Francisco, why do you look like a little mouse in disguise? You come in here and tell me that you have been talking to the people who own this import-export company. You tell me that they are not pleased with our earnings. Do they not know that we are in the middle of a great recession?

"I should have you thrown from the top of this building. Why did you not convince them that we are doing the best that we can? You are my account executive. Did I make a serious mistake when I gave you this position? You are my sister's husband. Were it not so, I would surely have you killed."

The little man stood trembling. He said nothing, as he knew the time was not right to reply to his superior. He wanted no part of the smuggling activities he had seen his brother-in-law become involved in. These illegal operations had now been going on for two years.

He was being told by the European parent company that they were not pleased with the absence of profit from their Guatemalan import-export operations. He had personally eliminated nearly thirty positions, trying to get the operations into a profitable position.

Francisco knew that everyone's days were numbered at the Guatemalan operations run by his brother-in-law, Hernando. He knew that his job, too, would soon be eliminated.

He was not sure, but he felt confident that the officials of the parent company would be furious if they found out what was going on in Guatemala. If the company were exposed, many of those people involved with Hernando would end up in prison.

His very own name, Francisco Hermes, was listed on all of the corporate documents and registrations. He was his company's chief accountant and controller of the Guatemalan corporation. And yes, he was Señor Banderas' brother-in-law.

His wife had forced him to come to work for her brother. The previous job that he had at the monastery did not pay half as much as he was now making, yet Francisco wished that he still had his previous job.

For some reason, his wife felt that her brother, Hernando, was a great man. She did not know that he had several women that he visited often and that he had not been faithful to her for several years. She also did not know that her brother had become a major player in the export of drugs to the United States as well as other European countries.

"Get out, you little weasel. You are nothing but trouble for me. Send in Garcia and Felipe. I need to talk to them right now." The two men to whom Hernando referred were sitting in a waiting area adjacent to the reception area. The two were extremely crude-looking characters to say the least. They both wore tailored black suits. Actually, their complete attire was black.

As the men entered Hernando's office, he waved them to one of the sitting areas and took a chair facing them. They both had an idea that perhaps things were not going well. They had watched many of their fellow employees clean out their desks, pack their belongings, and leave the premises.

Garcia and Felipe acted not only as Hernando's bodyguards, but they were also his muscle men. When dirty work needed to be done, it was assigned to either one of them or both of them. They both had reputations not just with their fellow employees, but also with the local authorities, identifying them as questionable characters.

"Francisco tells me that we are not doing as well as we should. He says that our people in Europe are not happy with our operations. What is happening? You tell me, why are we doing so poorly? Are we not moving enough products?"

Garcia looked at Felipe and motioned for him to reply to Hernando's question. Felipe was to be the one to provide the details as to why their income had dropped to the point where the people at the parent company were unhappy with their Guatemalan operations.

"Times are not good. We have not been pursing the import-export business. We have been doing as you directed; we have been working on acquiring the drugs you sell in the United States. In the drug business, we have many competitors. Our factories are not doing well because the other organizations have threatened our people. They say that we are no longer number one. The United States has great demand for more drugs, though.

"Our production is down because the people in the fields are being threatened as well. The Colombians have established a very good distribution program with their contacts in the United States."

"Who are these people that are threatening our people? Tell me who they are so that I can have them eliminated. I will not tolerate these people moving into my territory."

"They, too, are the Colombians. They do not scare easily. They are in control of their own government and are presently working on our elected officials. They have already killed Guatemala's head of finance. They are threatening to kill even the new president. Going up against the Colombians would not be wise. Perhaps we need to find another way to make money."

"What other ways could we make money, Felipe? We do not have any other resources. We abandoned the import-export business two years ago in order to concentrate on the drug trafficking. Do you have suggestions to make, or are you just providing me with excuses?"

Felipe responded, "The people in Belize tell us that they have great demand from the Arabian sheiks for young white women. They tell me that these Arabian sheiks will pay 380,000 quetzals for just one young female. That is 50,000 US dollars!

"The women must be between the ages of fifteen and twenty-five. They prefer blonde women. They say they will fly here in their jets and pick up the women. They want delivery of at least two women at a time."

"What are you waiting for? Put the word out to the people who work for us. Tell them that I will pay them 1000 quetzals for every woman that fits those requirements. Go to the tourist areas. Go wherever you have to. Find me some young, blonde women. Do it now!"

"We need to tell you more, Señor Banderas; we need to tell you what is happening in Florida."

"So tell me. What is it that you need to tell me, Felipe?"

Garcia' now responded to their demanding boss. Felipe nodded to Garcia to pick up the conversation and fill Hernando in on the details of what they had discovered. He was very close to the people who distribute the products in Florida.

"Si, Señor Banderas, much trouble is on the streets. Our people have complained that we are not providing them with enough products. They say that the demand is greater than we can deliver. Just as Felipe told you, our factories are not producing as much as the market in the United States is demanding. We are losing some of our better people to the Colombians

"I agree with Felipe. We would not be wise to go up against the Colombians. They are very dangerous people."

16

Amy stood exactly where she had been told to stand. She was about fifty feet from the cruise ship that was docking in front of her. About twenty people were milling around her, waiting to greet passengers disembarking from the cruise liner. Some were limousine drivers and others were tour bus representatives. She had sneaked in beside a tour bus director who flashed identification at the security guard as she passed through the gate. Amy waved and pointed to the woman ahead of her and was not challenged.

She was waiting for the gangplank to be lowered so that the passengers could come ashore. She held her small sign firmly in her hands and up against her torso. The sign would be held up high as soon as the passengers started coming ashore.

The sign had only numbers on it. The numbers were drawn with a thick pointed marker that made the numbers bold and easy to read.

Amy Creston, now twenty-two, was originally from Ohio. She had traveled to Ft. Lauderdale two years ago during the college spring break. She stood five-foot-six, had long blonde hair, and had maintained her figure. Her skin was darkly tanned, not only from being on the beach, but also living and sleeping on the beach.

She only had one friend, and that was George. Unfortunately, George had gotten her hooked on cocaine right after she arrived. She hadn't contacted her parents for over three months, as they had indicated that they wanted nothing to do with her. She begged and scrounged for food from the tourists, mostly men who wanted more than just a companion. She didn't get involved in prostitution as some of the other girls had. She was a junkie, and she knew it.

She had been told that she could not only make big money, as they described it, but she could also have an abundance of drugs. She knew deep down in her heart that she just could not sacrifice her body to satisfy her habit. She had been invited into using drugs but didn't realize that she would get hooked.

All she really wanted was enough food and drugs to survive from one day to the next. She had been picked up twice for possession but was released within a few hours because she had no record and the local jails were filled to capacity.

The gangplank was lowered and nearly a thousand people began to file down the ramp to the dock below. Some were being met by friends on the opposite side of the security fence and others were being met by tour buses. The cruise ship would not go out again for three days because the operators needed that long to replenish the ship's food supply and make ready all of the cabins. Besides, the crew would be given a twenty-four hour break.

Amy was holding her placard high over her head when a man appearing to be in his late forties approached her and identified himself as Diego.

"You must be Amy. Please follow me to the luggage area. I will have payment for you when I retrieve my luggage."

Amy obediently followed the man to where the passengers were picking up their luggage and working their way to the customs inspection area. The cruise ship had been on a one-week cruise to the Caribbean. Diego had boarded the ship in Belize. He walked over to two large suitcases and picked them up.

As he looked up, he observed two customs officials working the opposite end of the ramp with large German shepherd dogs. They were checking luggage as people exited through the narrow gate to the parking area. Diego was nervous and motioned for Amy to follow him. He walked slowly through the crowd in the opposite direction from the inspectors and the dogs.

Suddenly, he grabbed Amy by the arm and jerked her into a large empty container that had been unloaded and was waiting on the dock to be picked up. He pulled the door shut and then sat down, using one of his suitcases as a stool. He offered the other bag for Amy to sit on.

The heat inside the container was stifling. Diego removed his shirt and sat with sweat running down his chest and sides. Amy was also suffering. She was wearing a pair of short shorts and a halter top. The rest of her clothing was limited to a few more pieces of lingerie and two extra pair of shorts. All of her belongings were buried under a giant tree stump that served as a shelter for her and her friend George when the rain came down.

Originally, she had hung on to her suitcase. She had kept most of her belongings along with a few personal items in her one piece of luggage. Once, when she returned from working the beaches for food or money, she discovered the suitcase gone and only a few items of clothing strewn on the floor of the room she was now sharing with three other people.

Diego was staring at her, making her very nervous. She had stooped to just about everything, except sacrificing her body. That is where she drew the line. She was a junkie, but she wasn't a whore.

After thirty minutes passed, Diego opened the door slowly and peered down to the passenger exit gate that was now closed and probably locked. The customs officials had departed. He pushed open the door and felt the cool breeze from the bay as it cooled his body. Amy stepped out and stood still as the breeze blew over her.

"Follow me. I have a place near here. We can go out through that gate down at the end of the dock. Trucks will be using the same gate, so this should be easy."

"I just want to be paid so that I can go be with my friends. I don't want to go to your place."

"If you do not want to go to jail and if you want your money, then you will come with me. I do not want you as a *puta*. I am not interested in that."

Amy followed Diego against her better judgment. They walked past several people milling around the freight entrance. They were not stopped or questioned.

They had walked about two blocks when Diego turned into a short alley leading to what looked like an old store building. Using a key from his key ring, he unlocked a padlock attached to the front door. He opened the door and motioned for Amy to follow.

Once inside, he motioned for her to take a seat on the couch located against one of the walls. In addition to the couch was a relatively new flat screen TV on a small table, a chest of drawers, and a double bed. A door led into a small bathroom with a shower, sink, and toilet.

Diego opened his suitcases and began to pull out the back and bottom panels. Instantly, Amy saw what appeared to be about 50 kilos of what she knew and could easily identify as pure cocaine.

She desperately needed a fix. She hadn't had a hit since earlier in the day when she made the deal with her friend George. He had said that he told his people, as he called them, that Amy would meet Diego.

Diego picked up the phone and made two calls. Both times, he spoke in Spanish, which Amy did not understand. In a few minutes, a knock came at the door. Diego opened the door and was handed a large box containing a large pizza. He motioned for Amy to join him at his little table.

She hadn't eaten since the night before, and that was only half of a ham sandwich she had seen a girl toss into the trashcan a few feet from where she was sitting on a bench. As soon as the people were out of sight, she made a dash for the sandwich. She had some competition from an older guy standing about ten feet from the trashcan. He was another street person. Amy was the quickest and, therefore, got the sandwich remains.

About twenty minutes later came another knock at the door from two big and ugly men. They appeared to be in their late thirties or early forties. Diego gave them a large box containing the cocaine that he had smuggled in on the cruise ship.

One man grabbed the box containing the drugs, looked inside and then nodded to his partner. The other man opened a small brief case that contained bundles of

US $100 bills. He allowed Diego to reach in and move the bills around. He closed the case, handed it to Diego, and quickly headed out the door with his partner and the container of drugs.

Amy was sitting on the edge of the couch. She looked at Diego with pleading eyes and said, "Are you going to pay me with some of that money? I need to get going."

"Sorry, señorita, I am not going to give you any of these big bills. They do not belong to me. That was not our agreement. If you remember correctly, your friend George made arrangements for me to give you something better than money, if you would help me. I am going to give you something now that will make you *very* happy."

Knowing exactly what he meant, she watched him walk over to his chest of drawers, pull out the second drawer, and remove a small leather pouch. He opened the pouch, removed a syringe, a large spoon, and a cigarette lighter. He looked at her and grinned as he prepared the drug.

Amy paced the floor while she watched Diego preparing the drug. She was desperate; she kneeled down in front of him like a puppy and said, "Are you going to give me a hit right now? You have no idea how badly I need one."

"Yes, my little blonde bunny rabbit, I will give you a hit and then you can take a little nap. Soon, perhaps, I will let you go to your friends."

She wasn't watching him as he finished concocting the solution that was easily twice the dose she normally had. She wanted the hit, and she wanted it now. She was no longer hungry; she was desperate for the narcotic. She was shaking as she watched him.

Diego bent down, lifted her to her feet and squeezed her arm. He sought out a vein in between the many puncture marks covering the inside of her arm. As he shot the hot fluid into her veins, she immediately slumped to the floor.

He lifted her up and placed her on the couch. He knew that he had given her a large hit, and he also knew that she would sleep for about ten hours. He knew how this drug worked.

Amy loved the feelings that the drug had given her. She found herself in a euphoric state of bliss. She did not think about her compromised life, her family at home, or her future. All she thought about were things and experiences that made her feel good.

During the passing weeks, Amy had begun to realize that she never felt quite as wonderful as she had the first time she was introduced to the drug. No matter how often she would take the drug, it had less effect each time. Consequently, she found the need to have more and more of the drug in an attempt to get back that very first euphoric experience.

Diego walked over to the phone on his table and dialed a number. He heard several rings before a familiar voice came through on the other end of the line. He immediately recognized the voice of his superior, Hernando Banderas.

"Señor, this is Diego in Ft. Lauderdale. I have your money in my possession. I was also told by Felipe that you desire young blonde girls. Is that correct?"

"Yes, that is correct. What are you trying to tell me? Do you have a young girl for me? If you have a young girl, describe her to me."

"She tells me that she is twenty-two. She has blonde hair and a good figure. I have drugged her. I believe she is exactly what you are looking for."

"You said you drugged her? Will she be able to travel to Guatemala?"

"I believe that if I can keep her high, she will do whatever I ask. How should I get her to you?"

"I will send a plane. Be at Ft. Lauderdale Executive Airport at eleven tonight. You will have to arrive on time and get her on the plane. The plane will be talking to the control tower using a call sign of six-two-four Sierra. Listen on the aviation radio we have provided for you to use. The pilot will taxi toward hanger number 22, out of sight from the control tower. He will leave the engines running. The pilot will help you to get the girl to me here in Guatemala."

"Be quick and bring the girl and my money. Do not touch this girl. I want her to be unsoiled. If she is soiled, I will have both of you killed. Do you understand?"

17

"Mattie, I like your dad's plane much better than this plane," Alicia said. "His didn't bounce around so much. How much longer before we get to Guatemala City? I feel like we have been flying forever."

"According to my watch, we should arrive in about forty-five minutes. I have been reading about the city in this magazine. Do you know how big Guatemala City is? They have over two and a half million people living in the city. That's huge! They have lots of little towns near the city, but also have thick, dense jungles just a few miles from the city."

Bethany, sitting by the window, had been very quiet for several minutes. She had her hands tightly clasped together and appeared very tense. She looked over to Mattie, sitting in the middle of the three seats, and saw that she looked like she was totally relaxed. Alicia had her chair reclined as far as it would go and was staring at the plane's ceiling.

"Both of you seem to be really relaxed. I have to tell you that I am about as tense as a cat in a doghouse! I can't figure you two out. We are about to land in a foreign country, meet people we have never seen before, and commit ourselves to helping women and children who do not even speak our language."

"Beth, I think that Alicia and I have just about done all of the fretting that we can handle. We talked everything through a couple of hours ago while you were asleep.

"Personally, I think that all three of us could have ourselves in lather by the time we get to Charlene

Pearson's mission. Alicia and I have decided to kick back and go with the flow. I told Alicia that I agree with my dad's philosophy. Worrying is like paying premiums on an insurance policy you really don't need. In our case, our future is up to the Lord."

Bethany leaned over and kissed Mattie on the cheek. "Thanks, Mattie, I needed that. I'm going to lean back and, as you say, go with the flow. Maybe our friend has gone back to sleep. Her eyes are closed."

"Not sleeping. Praying. I wish this airliner would stop bouncing around like a ping-pong ball. If we don't land soon, I think I will be losing my dinner. Actually, when I think about it, it may be good to lose it. I thought the dinner was terrible. It tasted like cardboard that had been dipped into stale gravy," Alicia said.

"If you don't stop talking like that, I'll lose my dinner, too. I've been trying to not think about food. When I do think about food, I wonder what we will be eating when we are with Charlene," Mattie said as she leaned her seat back.

Two distinct chirps were heard as the American Airlines Boeing 737 touched down. The three girls were straining to see out of the small windows. La Aurora International Airport looked like most other airports. They taxied for what seemed like an eternity. When the front door of the aircraft was finally opened, people began to file down the aisle.

All three of the girls had taken Spanish in high school and were able to understand, in most cases, what was being said. Alicia commented that she was having a difficult time understanding some of the people as they seemed to talk very fast.

The girls worked their way through customs and immigration and then to the baggage claim area. As they approached the baggage carousels, they observed several people holding placards. Bethany jabbed Mattie in the side with her elbow and pointed to a short, skinny little man standing near the entrance.

The man appeared to be about five-foot-five. He was shorter that any of the three girls. He held a large piece of brown cardboard with the words "Multnomah Bible" written on it in black ink. The sign was not easy to read; however, the girls were convinced that this was the person who would greet them.

The three of them approached the short man, now wearing a big smile.

"Welcome, Señoritas. I am Pablo. Sister Pearson has asked me to meet you and take you to her home. Do you have your luggage?"

Mattie walked up to the little man and extended her hand towards him. "Hi, Pablo, I am Mattie Branson and this is Alicia Clark," she said as she pointed to Alicia, who also held her hand out to Pablo. "And this is Bethany Thomas."

"The answer to your question is, no, we do not have our luggage. I believe it will be coming on that first carousel that is moving around, the one where all of the people are standing."

All three of girls were confused when Pablo had referred to Charlene as "Sister." They knew that to be a common term used by the Catholic missions. They had believed that Charlene's mission was non-denominational and fundamental.

They picked up their backpacks, the only luggage they had brought with them, and followed

Pablo to a very old, dark green Ford van. The stretch-version van actually had four rows of seats and appeared to have been involved in several fender-benders, as there didn't appear to be a smooth surface anywhere on the vehicle. The windows were all rolled down since the car had no air conditioning. Mattie climbed into the front seat beside Pablo, while the two girls took to the row behind.

As they left the terminal area and worked their way down the crowded streets, the girls noted how people were everywhere. They walked in front of the car without any concern, and Pablo was constantly honking the horn. This action seemed to have very little effect on the people jay-walking across the streets.

Pablo indicated that they would need the better part of an hour to reach the mission, as the drive to Charlene's mission would take them out of the city. The terrain was partially rolling hills with a few fields of some kind of produce. A large portion of the land surrounding their travels to the mission appeared to be rainforest. The undergrowth was very thick. Occasionally, they would see an opening with a cleared field and a small farm. Pablo indicated that he was not familiar with what the people were growing.

They saw a few modest houses along the road, most with animals running free in their small fenced yards. The girls were chatting back and forth, spotting several goats, a few pigs, and a multitude of chickens. Every now and then, they would see a more prosperous spread with cows in a pasture and horses in a corral.

Pablo was quiet as he drove. Traffic was sparse, and in some cases they had the entire road to themselves. Eventually, Pablo turned down a road that had been paved at one time, but now was badly broken up and full of deep holes. The road would have been much more easily navigated if it were not partially surfaced.

They soon left the area that was partially inhabited and traveled another seven kilometers until they reached a small village.

Although Charlene's mission was said to be only a little over 50 kilometers from the airport, the ride took them nearly an hour before they pulled up in front of a run-down-looking, adobe two-story building. Pablo jumped out of the car and ran around to open all of the doors for the girls.

A tall slender lady came through the front entrance of the building and held out her arms to the girls. She gave each girl a big hug and said numerous times, "Welcome, welcome."

Charlene Pearson was about the same height as the girls, nearly five-foot-seven. Because she wore her graying hair tied back in a bun and had deep wrinkles indicating that she had led a difficult life, her age was difficult to peg. The girls estimated she was in her late thirties or early forties. She was thin, her features were drawn, and she wore a simple blue cotton print dress.

As Charlene led them into the building, they passed through a classroom with desks and chairs located on both sides of the room with no particular order to the way the desks were positioned. A large blackboard hung on one wall and numerous hand-drawn pictures were on the opposite wall.

On the other side of the room was a large arch that served as the entrance to a courtyard that held several benches and a small circular fountain that had no water. Two stairways, one on each end of the courtyard, led to the second story. The girls observed at least ten young children leaning over the steel rails or sitting on the steps that led to the upper floor.

Charlene led them up one of the staircases, down a short hall, and into a room that held three single beds and one large chest of drawers. A large rod extended on each side of the entrance that would service as a place to hang clothing with about ten wire hangers on each rod. She motioned for the girls to deposit their backpacks on one of the beds and follow her.

A large oak door was at the end of the hall that had a sign with the word "toilet." Charlene knocked twice on the door and then opened it. The bathroom had two sinks, one toilet, and one metal shower stall without a door or a curtain.

"I'm sorry, ladies, but this is the best that we have. I know that we are really very primitive. This is better than some places. Many homes have no inside plumbing whatsoever. By now, I am sure you are aware that this is a very humble facility."

Charlene led them around her facility and showed them the rooms where she taught classes as well as a fairly large eating area. All told, the facility had eight sleeping rooms. Four rooms are reserved for single women or women with children. The remaining four rooms were dormitory type rooms for children. The children were separated by age and gender. They had rooms for the boys and rooms for the girls. Currently, three single women were at the mission plus fourteen orphaned children.

The courtyard was the primary playground for the smaller children; the older kids played soccer and other games in the vacant field behind the mission.

Two young girls in their early teens had been at the mission for nearly four years. They were not from the same family, but they had come from the same village. They were not happy girls; they were sullen and very rarely talked about their lives. Charlene had tried to reach them, but to no avail. Their pasts were so horrible and had left scars on their minds that just wouldn't go away.

These two girls helped with the little children. They bathed the little ones and washed most of their clothes. An old wringer-type washing machine was still running and a double sink in a makeshift laundry room.

A clothes line was behind the building that served as a drying place for all of the laundry. Teenagers were assigned to watch the drying clothes so that some of the articles would not mysteriously disappear. The teenaged girls also helped with the cleaning, which Charlene said was a continuous chore.

The previous women assisting Charlene were both gone. One had gone home on leave in order to satisfy the U.S. State Department requirements, and the other made the decision to return to her family home in California.

When they had finished their tour, Charlene suggested that the girls take some time to get unpacked and freshen up. She suggested if they had any valuables, they should bring them to her office where she had a small safe that was bolted to the concrete floor. She told them that although they hadn't faced any problems recently, some of the older kids dropped off at her mission had a habit of stealing whatever they wanted.

The girls walked back to their assigned room and unpacked the few items they had brought with them. They placed most of their things in one of the drawers of the single chest of drawers. Mattie chose the third drawer and Alicia chose the top drawer. This left the middle drawer for Bethany. They all agreed that the bottom drawer would be reserved for soiled clothing ready for the laundry.

The girls ate lunch with all of Charlene's people. The lunch consisted of tortillas, red beans, and rice. Charlene told the girls that they needed to get used to this diet, as what they were eating was pretty much a staple meal to the people of Guatemala. Charlene said that they had a small garden the kids managed located behind the building. She added that, occasionally, they would have chicken or pork.

The children laughed, talked, and most of the time stared at the three young blonde girls who had come to live with them. They all spoke Spanish. Charlene spoke only English when she was talking with the girls. One of the older women spoke some English; however, she preferred to speak in her native tongue, Spanish.

When lunch was finished, Charlene asked the three girls to come into her office. She closed the door behind her and took a seat behind an old oak desk that had seen better days.

"I really need to brief the three of you about our community and how we are viewed by these people. They are mostly all Catholic with a few Protestants.

Although some are very dedicated Christians, some are very evil people here who claim they are Christians.

"Over the years, I have been able to present Jesus Christ to many. I am sad to say that, though, only a few have taken Jesus into their hearts and chosen to serve only Him.

"Remember, we are nondenominational. That is to say that we do not bombard them with our beliefs. If you feel led to witness to someone, share only what the Lord has done in *your* life. If they want to learn more, let them come to us here. We have Bibles provided to us by the Wycliffe Bible Translator organization. If someone is interested, we give them away. They are free."

Mattie said, "Pablo referred to you as Sister Pearson. Isn't that strange if you're not Catholic?"

"Pablo came to us from a Catholic Convent. That's a habit for him to call me Sister. He accepted the Lord two months after I found him sitting on my front stoop. He is now my driver and my maintenance man. He really is good at fixing things. I don't know what I would do without him."

123

18

The taxiing twin-engine King Air aircraft came into view as it approached the area where Diego was standing with the young blonde girl leaning against his shoulder. As he had been directed, Diego pointed his small pencil-sized flashlight at the taxiing plane.

The pilot stopped the King Air about 50 feet from where Diego was standing and left the engines running. A few seconds later, Diego observed the side door open. He quickly pushed the blonde girl toward the plane and the open door. He motioned for the pilot to help him drag the young girl into the aircraft. The pilot forced the barely conscious girl into one of the back seats and fastened her seat belt. He closed the door to the King Air and motioned for Diego to follow him to the front cockpit.

The pilot, who was accustomed to this sort of activity, spoke professionally into his microphone, "Executive tower, this is King Air six-two-four Sierra, taxiing for takeoff. Please activate my flight plan to Houston."

The plane would never arrive in Houston, as the pilot, once airborne, would call in on a different frequency, cancel the flight plan, and state that he was proceeding to an alternate, uncontrolled airport. The numbers that the pilot used belonged to a courier flight service stationed in Houston, Texas. Being dark, the control operator would not be able to see the numbers displayed on the side of the King Air. They did not correspond with the numbers the pilot had provided.

THE VILLA

This was a standard routine that had been used many times without discovery or incident. One of his people located in Houston had filed a flight plan from Houston to Fort Lauderdale, providing the exact time that the plane would arrive at the Florida airport. Banderas' plane actually took off from Guatemala City. It flew very low, only a few feet from the water, to avoid being detected by coastal radar. It flew directly to a small Caribbean island not far from the east Texas coast. The plane refueled and flew again at a very low altitude directly to Ft. Lauderdale.

The control tower would be expecting a flight from Houston using those identification numbers and wouldn't question the King Air when it called for landing instructions.

The fully fueled aircraft would once again fly for a few miles in the direction of Houston. Then, the pilot would drop down very close to the water and fly directly to Guatemala City.

The King Air flew only a few feet from the water for nearly an hour. Then, the pilot climbed to 12,000 feet and engaged the autopilot coupled to the navigation system. The pilot stated that it was exactly 1,000 miles from airport to airport. He went on to add that this aircraft was equipped with extra long-range fuel tanks providing up to seven hours of flight time, or an approximate range of 1,400 miles.

The air had been bumpy near the water; however, now that they were flying above the clouds, everything was relatively smooth. Diego leaned back, closed his eyes, and fell asleep.

* * *

"Hey, what's going on? Where are we? Why am I in this airplane? Where are you taking me?"

Diego awoke at the sound of the shouting girl. He turned and looked back at the young girl who had come out of her former drugged state.

"The best thing for you to do is to be quiet and wait until we land. Don't ask any more questions. Then, and only then, will I tell you where you are going."

"I got you your drugs. I saw you get your money. What more do you want from me?"

"I said for you to be quiet. We will be flying for another two hours. You would be wise to go back to sleep."

As tough as she thought she was, Amy began to silently weep. They couldn't hear her in the front of the airplane, but she sobbed for a long time until she had literally drained herself of all emotion. She thought about her friend in Florida, and then she thought about her family in Ohio.

She didn't know why she considered George her friend. Actually, other than a few street people that she had met on the beach, George was the only one she knew. Truth be told, he is the one who got Amy hooked on drugs. Then he had forced her to be a courier for him. For that, George kept her supplied with only enough cocaine to keep her under his control.

As the plane continued on its trip to Guatemala, she thought of what had happened to her life. She had been an A student in college and would have graduated this year. Amy had called her father and told him that she had gotten into trouble. She confessed that she was hooked on drugs and asked for his help. Because he had originally forbidden her to go to Florida for the spring break, he told her she was now on her own. He said he didn't care what would happen to her. She tried to talk to her mother, but her father would not allow it.

Amy fell asleep and then woke up when she heard the landing gear come down and then the wheels touch the runway. She sat up in her seat and looked out of the small window at her side. She saw lights everywhere. She watched as the aircraft taxied down the runway and then turned directly into a hangar. She heard the large overhead door close and then the aircraft door came open.

Felipe stood below the steps, peered into the plane and saw Amy. He grinned and then he extended his arm through the door opening.

"Come with me my little blonde baby doll. I will take you to where you will live until we decide who you will be with."

"I don't want to go anywhere with you or any of your friends. I want to go back to where you forced me into this airplane."

"Hey, Diego, you have brought us a feisty one. We will have to teach her some manners before we send her to someone."

Garcia, Felipe's partner, looked at the young girl and said, "Give her to me for a few days. I will not only teach her some manners, I will teach her how to make love."

"Amigo, Mr. Banderas would not like that. He wants this little butterfly to be untouched and pure. He says she will bring more money if she is not soiled. We had better take her to Señora Coronado as Mr. Banderas has directed."

Amy quickly determined that trying to run would prove futile. She had no idea where she was and, furthermore, no idea as to what these men were planning to do with her.

"Her eyes are all puffed up and her pupils are dilated. Diego, what have you done to this girl. Is she on drugs?"

"Si, Señor Felipe, she was the addict that my contact sent to meet me when I got off the boat from Belize. I talked to Mr. Banderas and described her. He told me to bring her. She has not had any drugs now for almost ten hours. Should we provide her with something now so that she will be calm?"

"Let me call Mr. Banderas. He will tell us what he wants us to do with her."

Felipe took out his cell phone and punched in a familiar number. He walked around the inside of the hangar as he talked on the phone. The conversation ended, and he hung up.

"Mr. Banderas says that we are to take her to the house of Isabella Coronado. He says she will know what to do with her."

One of the building attendants pushed a button, and the giant overhead door opened. A black late model Mercedes pulled into the hangar and stopped in front of the small group standing beside the plane. The driver, named Juan, got out and walked over to the group.

"Mr. Banderas wants you to take this young girl to Señora Coronado's plantation outside of the city. He wants her there quickly. That means you do not stop for anything. Do you understand?"

THE VILLA

"Si, Señor. I will not stop for anything. Señora Coronado's plantation is about an hour away. Please tell Mr. Banderas that I am on my way."

The Mercedes driver pulled out of the hangar with Amy, still clad in only short shorts and a halter top, seated in the middle of the back seat.

Nearly an hour later, the car stopped in front of a large, well maintained, three-story villa. Architecturally the huge three-story villa resembled the renaissance era. The picturesque structure looked much like the spectacular Relais of France.

When the big Mercedes stopped, an older woman in her mid-forties walked up to the car and held out her hand for Amy. She smiled and said, "Welcome to Villa de las Flores, my home. What is your name, pretty lady?"

"My name is Amy, and I don't know where I am. Where have these men brought me? Why am I here? What are you going to do to me?"

"Let me take you to your room so that you can rest. No one is going to harm you.

"In answer to your first question, you are in Guatemala City, located in Central America. You are at the Villa de las Flores plantation. Translated to English, it is known as 'Home of the Flowers.'

"You are the guest of Señora Isabella Coronado. That is me. I live alone in this house with my servants. My family has owned this plantation for nearly two centuries. I am not certain why you are here."

19

Garrett didn't usually ride right up to the fence circling the back of the ranch house. Dan was standing at the kitchen sink when he saw him. Garrett's horse was covered with lather and appeared to have been ridden hard.

Dan walked out the back door of the ranch house, meeting Garrett halfway to the fence.

"What's going on, Garrett? You look like you've been riding hard."

"I have, boss. I got to the ranch in a little over two hours. I went up to check on the herd, and the two guys we got watching them. I just about did my horse in getting back here. Old Ned really hung in there. He hasn't worked like this for a long time. He's not that old, but I pushed him pretty hard.

"I got some bad news. Our two guys heard a couple of motorbikes in the middle of the night. They are camped right where Andy set up camp. As soon as they heard the sounds, our two guys said they saddled up and went out to check the herd.

"Actually the herd was all around them, but apparently a few were down by an old abandoned fire-road we didn't know existed. We don't usually ask them to stay in the saddle during the night. The herd doesn't move around that much at night."

"You're right, Garrett. They did just like we expected them to. Their job is just to keep an eye on the herd and move them around during the day to where the grass is. Sounds like we had some rustlers checking the herd."

"They weren't just checking, boss. They must have had a rig because I saw truck tire marks on the fire-road. We think we're missing a few, perhaps six calves. That's a guess because we haven't made a complete herd count."

"I can't believe they would raid the herd this early in the summer! Those calves are still pretty small. You say they had a truck?"

"Best I can tell they had a pickup with a ramp. We could see where they loaded and then turned around. That fire-road hasn't been used for years. It actually runs into the designated wilderness area. I didn't even know it existed until the guys showed me. It doesn't appear to even be on the Forest Service maps. What do you think we ought to do? Do you want to go back up there?"

"I'll give the county sheriff a call, and then I'll put a call into the Cattleman's Association. This has to be stopped quickly. I'll talk to the authorities. I know they will want to go up there. In the meantime, get hold of the Forest Service and see if they don't have some old maps that would show that fire-road."

"If we can get a map, we can take the Jeep and the authorities up to where they rustled our calves. We'll have to get special permission to take a vehicle into the wilderness area."

Jessie was staring out the kitchen window and could tell that something serious was going on. She looked at Garrett's horse and saw him covered with white lather. She had seen horses that had been ridden hard, but not with this much lather on them. She turned as Dan walked into the house with a worried look on his face.

THE VILLA

"What's going on, Dan? What's Garrett been doing? Ned, his horse looks like he is ready to drop."

"He's been up checking the herd. Some rustlers came in during the night and took a few of our calves. He rode hard all the way back here to bring me the news. I need to go and call Sheriff Simpson and tell him what's going on."

"Is he still the sheriff? I thought he retired. He's got to be getting pretty old."

"He's only a couple of years older than me, sweetheart. He says that he won't run again. He still has a couple of years to serve."

Dan turned and walked down the hallway to his office and dialed the bold number emblazoned on the back of the telephone directory.

"Hey Bob, this is Dan Branson. I think I have a pretty serious problem to tell you about."

"What's the deal, Dan? You planning to run off again to some distant land and catch bad guys?"

"No, Bob, this is serious. We had our herd hit by some rustlers last night. They appear to have taken a few of our calves. They went in on a fire-road that we didn't even know existed.

"I have Garrett trying to get ahold of an old map that might list where the road takes off from. I'll need to get permission to drive the Jeep up there. I'd like you to have at least one of your investigators go up with us to see if they left behind any clues."

"Dan, hold tight until you hear from me. I will get ahold of the Cattlemen's Association and bring them into the picture. I will probably call the feds, too. They usually get involved in this sort of thing because sometimes these guys cross state lines."

"This is really bizarre stuff you are telling me. I thought that sort of thing died with the Old West. I know pirates roam the seas, but I can't imagine cattle rustlers in this day and age."

Dan turned to see Jessie standing in the doorway with Garrett standing right behind her. Danny was peeking around Garrett to see what was going on. Dan stood up and motioned for everyone to come into his office.

"Looks like I had better fill you in on what's going on. I talked to Bob Simpson. He's going to contact the Cattlemen's Association and also the feds. He says that sometimes these guys try to cross state lines. We're not supposed to do anything until we hear from him.

"Let's all go into the kitchen and wait for his call. I think we had better develop a plan to support our guys at the mountain camp," Dan motioned.

"Is this going to be a dangerous thing? Should our guys have guns to protect themselves? Will the rustlers come back for more of our calves? Will a lot of shooting take place?" Danny inquired with a mix of nervousness, anxiousness, and excitement.

"Danny Boy, you ask way too many questions. I doubt that the guys will come back. Most likely they are long gone. I'd really be surprised if they catch them."

"Dan, I talked to Ed Hansen over at the Forest Service," Garrett said. "He's looking through all of the old charts that they have of the Cascades. He thinks he remembers a fire-road that goes nearly to the base of North Sister. It was cut around 1920 when they had a huge fire that went all the way to the crest of the mountains. Since they established the wilderness areas, they don't have any maps that show any roads beyond the limits of the boundaries."

"Thanks, Garrett. That will help if they can find that map. In the meantime, let's come up with a plan. We need to support our two guys, Craig Terrell and Mark Carmine, up at the camp."

"Actually, they seem to be OK. They felt bad because they knew that their job was to watch the herd. I think I convinced them that they couldn't have done anything to stop them."

* * *

"Dad, a green car just drove up in front of the house with a police car right behind it."

They all moved to the front door and saw a man in a brown suit getting out of a green sedan with Forest Service markings on the door. The man in the police car was not in uniform and stepped out of his vehicle, joining the other man. Together they walked up to the front door.

"Hey Branson; good to see you. I would like to introduce you to Stan Peterson, the district supervisor for the Forest Service over in Bend. You probably recognize his face from all of the publicity they get in the Bend Bulletin."

Stan Peterson's picture had been in the local newspapers several times during the past few months regarding a great deal of controversy pertaining to the regulations and restrictions that apply to people traveling into the wilderness areas of the Oregon Cascades.

"Hello, Bob. Thanks for the quick response to my call. Mr. Peterson, good to meet you. I have heard a lot about you. Won't you both please come in? I believe we have a lot to talk about."

Stan introduced himself to Jessie, Garrett, and Danny. Bob announced that an all-points bulletin was sent out to every law enforcement agency in the state. Dan motioned for the group to take seats on the leather couches.

Danny took a seat on the fireplace hearth and watched his dad, mom, and Garrett as they took seats on one of the leather couches. Sheriff Simpson sat down beside Mr. Peterson, who was first to speak.

"First let me say that my name is Stan, not Mr. Peterson. I want to apologize for all of the publicity that Sheriff Simpson referred to. I must also tell you that I have heard a great deal about the Branson family and your Triple Peaks Ranch. I have never been here, but now that I have, I can attest to what I have heard. This is truly a spectacularly beautiful location. I have also heard much about you, Sheriff Simpson.

"Let me hand you a map one of our people located that shows the old fire-road you referred to. We are authorizing both of you to use the road to get to the location of this alleged crime. As you know, we've been extremely dry, and we need you to be very cautious with your vehicles. If you don't mind, I need to get back to my office. Good luck finding the perpetrators."

20

Bob Simpson got up and reached for Stan's hand. "Thanks for taking the time to meet with us. You can be assured that we will all be careful when we enter your forest. I know that you broke some rules and made a special concession when you provided us with this map and your approval for us to drive a vehicle in the wilderness area."

"Dan, I'll need one of my detectives to accompany Dan and me when we drive up there this afternoon. Isn't that old Jeep you have parked out in the round barn a station wagon? Will it run?"

Danny excitedly joined the conversation, "Sheriff Simpson, it runs good. It has a V8 engine. I just drove it yesterday. Dad lets me drive around the ranch. I can't go on the roads because I am not old enough to get a driver's license. It has a fifty-gallon gas tank, two batteries, and two fuel pumps. It's really old, but it runs good. It can go anywhere. My sister used it to learn how to drive. I'm using it for the same reason."

Everyone had smiles on their faces as they listened to Danny describe the old brown Jeep station wagon parked out in the round barn.

Dan, who had been silent, nodded as Danny was describing the old Jeep and agreed that it would be the best vehicle to take up the old road.

Stan bid everyone goodbye and said he had to return to his office. Bob stood up and said he would go out to his patrol car and radio for his detective to meet them here at the ranch. He said that he knew he was in his car and probably not far away.

Danny looked at his dad with pleading eyes, knowing that an adventure was about to begin. He wanted to go with them when they drove up to where the rustlers had loaded the calves.

Jessie walked over to Danny and put her arm around him and said, "I guess you know that the Jeep only has room enough for four men. Garrett will be going up the mountain with your dad, the sheriff, and the detective. With all of these bad guys roaming around, I would like to have you stay here with me. I may need you."

"Shucks, I could easily ride on the top of the Jeep. It has big racks up there."

"Not this time, Danny Boy. I need you to stay here and look after your mom."

Garrett stood up and said he would pull the Jeep up to the gas pump and make sure it was full. The men walked out to where Garrett was cleaning the windows on the old Jeep.

Just then, they saw another man dressed in a black suit approaching the group.

"Hi, Mitch, this is Dan Branson, and this is Garrett Sounders. Take your jacket off and leave it here. Dan and Garrett are going to drive us up to where the bad guys loaded up the calves. Guys, this is Mitch Martin, my lead detective. I'm going to ask him to play Sherlock Holmes when we get to the spot where the rustlers did their deed. He'll see if he can find a few clues that might aid us in our investigation."

All four men climbed into the old brown Jeep. Garrett sat beside Dan in the passenger seat, acting as the navigator. They had just reached the main intersection of the highway that led to the mountain passes. Garrett was studying the map, and he pointed to the road going up the South Santiam and continued to run his finger along a line. Dan followed his signal and turned left onto the highway.

"Turn into the Jacobs' place. We need to go back across his property to the old dry wash. I think that's where we are going to find the beginning of the old fire-road," Garrett said.

They stopped to see Ed Jacob and readily got his permission to cross the property. Dan said the old Jeep was accustomed to driving through the brush. They found the dry wash and quickly found the signs of an old road that had recently been traveled.

The four men in the old brown Jeep wound their way up the abandoned road that was leading them up into the mountains. Although they could tell that someone had driven the road recently, they saw several places following the rustlers' tire marks that they had to divert from the road in order to circumnavigate large, fallen trees.

Clearly, the rustlers had made at least two trips up the old road. Tire marks were in the soft soil from the motorbikes coming back down the mountain.

About twenty minutes into their journey, they found a fair-sized clearing by the tire marks, as though a lot of activity took place at this particular spot. They all got out of the Jeep. Dan and Garrett were asked to stay with the Jeep so that they wouldn't accidently disturb any of the marks or potential evidence that the sheriff and his detective might locate in the clearing.

Mitch began walking from side to side through the area. About 10 minutes after they had stopped, and called to Bob, standing with Dan and Garrett, and motioned the three of them to where he was standing.

"Guys, I am sure that they came up this fire-road on their motorbikes before they brought the trucks up here. My guess is—and I think I'm right—they had probably ridden the bikes down that old wash from one of the more heavily used roads and then drove up the wash until they located the old abandoned road. Looks to me like they did a great deal of research and planning before they came up here to grab some of the Triple Peaks' calves," Mitch offered. "I would say that they didn't try to bring the trucks up here until they had pretty well established a route. I bet if we followed this wash a short distance, we would find where they turned off of the regular fire-road, drove up the wash, and then up the road that takes off from Jacob's place. I don't believe you could see that wash from the Jacob's house or barns.

"This place where we are standing is where they left the truck that carried, according to my calculations, the three bikes. According to what I see, they brought the trucks in here, probably a day or two before they pulled the job. I figure we are looking at three of them," Mitch continued. "I can also confirm by the tire marks that we're dealing with three bikes. The bikes were driven ahead of the guy driving the truck, right up to Dan's herd. I doubt they took more than a couple of minutes to cut the calves out of the herd and drive them up the ramp on the back of their pickup."

"If I hear you correctly, you say you think that these guys came up here a couple of days before they actually went up this road and grabbed some of my calves?" Dan stated.

"Yes, Dan, that's what I think. I could be wrong, but I am pretty sure that some of these tire tracks are two or three days old. I can tell you that the ones from last night look very fresh. I figure that they scouted out the fire-road according to an old map, like the one you have, planned their job, and then laid low for maybe two or three days. I think that once they figured out how they were going pull this job, they brought the two trucks up here, left them, and then laid low until they were sure no one had seen them driving the trucks up the old wash."

Garrett spoke next. "Mitch, you have impressed me. I don't see how you can tell all of that by just wandering around this here clearing. So what we may be looking at are three guys that might have hung around Sisters for a couple of days. Am I right?"

"Actually, I think you are right on." Mitch said. "I believe that we need to check all of the motels in Sisters and see if they had three guys riding bikes that stayed for one or two nights. Boss, do you want me to bring some guys into town to do this or should I do the inquiries?"

"No Mitch, I think I'm going to leave the whole investigation up to you. If you need help, ask for it. Otherwise, get back to me if you discover anything in town."

The four men climbed back into the Jeep and continued up the abandoned road for nearly an hour. Rounding a bend in the road, they reached another clearing that showed the tire marks of not one, but two trucks, going back and forth, obviously turning around.

"I'm pretty sure that this is the spot where they herded the calves down the road and into their truck. If you look right here, you can see where the hoofprints stop. See the line in the ground? That was probably made by the ramp on the back of the truck," Mitch commented.

All of them stood back listening to Mitch and looking at the marks in the ground that he was referring to. The decision was made that they had enough evidence as to how the rustlers got into the mountains and how they went back out. They headed back down the old abandoned road and back to the dry wash. They drew the conclusion that Mitch was correct and that the dry wash was the way that the rustlers accessed the old road.

They had been driving slowly for about thirty minutes when Bob's portable radio began to page him.

"This is Bob."

"Bob, this is dispatch. The State Police got your guys. They stopped them as they were pulling out of a motel near Biggs junction. They have two pickups, one with three motorbikes in the back, and the other with five calves. They want to know what to do with the calves."

"Tell them to give them some water and some hay. Ask them to come up with a plan on how to get them back to my ranch," Dan said as he let out a big sign of relief.

"This is a nice drive, but I think we need call it a day. What do you think, partner?" Bob Simpson asked his detective.

21

Amy opened her eyes and stared at the ceiling above her. "How beautiful," she thought. "I know I am not in Heaven, but those are angels painted on the ceiling." She was staring up at a painting on the ceiling of white billowing clouds against a pale, light blue sky. The painting was breathtaking with angels flying around the clouds everywhere.

She examined her surroundings. She was lying in the middle of a huge bed that felt like it had a feather mattress. She was covered with an equally large, down-filled comforter. She could not remember being in such luxury—ever.

The room was also enormous, totaling almost 300 square meters. The tile floor had numerous oriental carpets scattered throughout the room. The furniture was massive to fit the room. Several tapestry-covered chairs, a long lounge, a vanity, and dressing table that matched the rest of the furniture were in the room.

She climbed out of bed and walked to one of the floor-to-ceiling drapery-covered windows. She pushed back the draperies and found herself looking out at lawns, shrubbery, and flowers in every direction. Numerous pathways seemed to lead in different directions. Further out toward the middle of the gardens was a giant statue of a Castilian knight standing majestically on top of a waterfall of cascading waters.

She walked over to the vanity table and looked at herself in the mirror. She was wearing a full-length cotton nightgown. She scanned the entire room but could not locate the clothing she had been wearing for the past several days.

Amy turned when she heard the latch turn and the door open. A woman, whom she vaguely remembered meeting the night before, stepped into the room. She set a tray on the small table located in the center of the room.

Isabella Coronado was a stately woman. She stood tall and erect. She appeared to be about five-foot-seven tall, with short gray hair. She looked to be in her mid-forties and had taken good care of herself. She was neither overweight nor skinny. She was well proportioned and well groomed. She walked across the room in a strong and confident manner.

"Good morning, Amy. Did you sleep well? You appeared completely exhausted last night when you were brought to me."

"Where am I? Why have I been brought here? Who are these people who kidnapped me?" What is going to happen to me?"

"Eat the food I have prepared for you. Then, you will want to bathe. I have ordered a bath drawn for you. Go through that large blue door," Isabella said as she pointed to the blue door located in the far corner of the room. "When you have finished bathing, you will find some suitable clothes in the tall cabinet next to the vanity table."

When she had finished giving instructions to Amy, she calmly turned and left the room. Amy did not hear the latch turn. She walked over to the door and tried the knob. The door swung open, revealing a long, wide hallway with several doors on each side.

"Good morning, Miss Amy. I have brought you some towels," a woman dressed in a light blue uniform said as she walked past Amy, then continued across the room and entered the room through the blue door.

Amy, following closely behind, was again studying her surroundings. She followed the woman through the door and into the large bathroom. The room was larger than she had imagined it could be. In the center of the room was what looked like a pond. It was the size of many modern bedrooms and was filled with swirling warm water. The woman in the uniform set the towels on a small, marble-covered table and faced Amy. "Miss Amy, would you like me to assist you while you bathe?"

Amy did not verbally answer. She shook her head "no," indicating that she wanted to be alone.

She spent a short time soaking in the massive tub, trying to figure out what was taking place in her life. Finally, she stepped out of the water and dried herself. She wrapped a bath sheet around her body and walked back into the bedroom.

She opened the tall cabinet Isabella had referred to and went through the hanging garments. She chose a yellow cotton dress that looked like it had never been worn. She opened one of the drawers below the hanging clothes and found several pieces of undergarments. Amazingly, everything was her size, and everything fit perfectly.

When she was fully dressed and had dried and combed her hair, she stood in front of the mirror that covered the inside of the door of the tall cabinet. She almost didn't recognize herself. She had been so used to seeing herself as a 'beach bum,' she couldn't believe the transformation. Her complexion was good but her eyes had the telltale black rings that proved that she was still a junkie. She needed a fix bad. Besides that—not knowing it to be a symptom of withdrawal—she was hungry.

She was startled when she heard someone behind her. "Now you look radiant. Let's go for a little walk. I will try to answer some of your questions."

Isabella led her down to the main floor and out through the French doors at the back of the villa and into the gardens.

"First, I must tell you who I am and what I do. As you have already been told, this is a very large estate. Actually, this is a plantation. It is no longer productive, but for twenty years, my deceased husband and I grew mangos and pineapples in the fields beyond the tall trees you see at the back of the gardens. My husband, Julius, died when he was only forty-two. We inherited this plantation from my husband's father. The plantation belonged to his father before him.

"My mother died when I was a teenager while I was away at school in Spain. I have no other brothers or sisters. Julius was killed in a plane crash. He had gone to visit his mother in Bolivia but never returned to me. I have never considered remarrying.

"My husband's father was one of the first and largest investors in the Consolidated International Trading Corporation. Because of that large investment, I receive a substantial payment each month.

"Señor Banderas, the man who sent you to me, is currently in charge of the company's Guatemalan division. I didn't like it that Señor Banderas was getting involved in trafficking drugs. I am opposed to such things, but I do not say anything because I know going against such a big man and his very wicked associates is not wise.

"I have never been involved with what he is doing. I think that it is wrong. I am not sure what his plans are for you, but I can guess. I don't like it.

"I receive enough money each month from his company to keep my home and my servants. Before my husband died, he told me that we would always receive substantial sums from the company from his father's investment. Unfortunately, these are the same people who Señor Banderas is working for.

"I have never questioned the circumstances. I occasionally house one of Señor Bandera's guests for a few days. I rarely see him or any of his people. When I received his phone call, he told me you would be with me for a week or maybe two."

"What do you think he is going to do with me? How long before I will be taken away?" Amy asked.

"I don't like to tell you this, but from what I have heard, the bigger crime cartels are beginning to force Señor Banderas out of the drug business. I believe that someone has told him that 'white slavery' is a profitable venture. I think that you are to be the first.

"I have been told beautiful blonde girls like you are in high demand from the Arabian sheiks. I believe that he is searching for more girls. They don't want to come here for less than two girls."

Amy's complexion turned white, her knees trembled, and then she staggered. If not for Isabella, she would have fallen to the ground. She stumbled over to a concrete bench and sat down. Instantly, she began to weep. Isabella sat down beside her, put her arm around her and pulled her close to her. She ran her hand over Amy's soft blonde hair and rested her chin on top of her head.

"I had a daughter. Her name was Sophia. She died when she was only three. She had been bitten by a poisonous snake while playing in the fields while her father and I were working with our harvesters. We left the fields and have never grown fruit since that day.

"I don't know if I can help you, but I will try to see what I can do to stop him from sending you away. He is a very wicked man."

Amy looked into Isabella's eyes. "I don't want to go to Arabia. I need drugs. Can you get me some drugs? I really need a fix."

"No, my beautiful lady. I do not have any drugs. I will not get you any drugs either. I am going to help you get free of that awful stuff. Just trust me and do everything I tell you, and you will soon be well. Where is your home? Where is your family? Will they be looking for you?"

"I no longer have a home. I left my home to go to Florida to be with my friends. My friends left me behind when they discovered that I had been using drugs. I called my father for help, but he told me he would not help and that I no longer had a home. I didn't want to become an addict, but a new friend got me started. At first I thought it was good. Then I found out I couldn't quit."

Isabella continued to hug Amy as the two sat on the bench for several more minutes. Finally, Amy rose from the bench and said, "I think I would like to go back to my room. I am still very tired. Can I go back to my room now?"

"Yes, I can take you to your room. First, I need for you to tell me how much drugs you are used to taking each day."

"Yesterday was the most I have ever had. That man who brought me here gave me a shot that knocked me out for hours. Normally, I am lucky if I get a hit every three or four days."

"Did you eat the food I brought to your room?"

"Yes, but I am still very hungry. My appetite is going crazy. I don't understand what is going on with my body. Could I possibly have a sandwich?"

"I will take you to your room, and you can rest. I will bring you some more food."

* * *

Hernando Banderas dialed Isabella's number and waited for her to answer. "How is the girl doing? What do we need to do to detoxify her so that she will be of some value to me?"

"The girl is going to be fine. You cannot rush this. She is not hooked badly; however, I will need some time. She should be well in perhaps a couple of weeks. You must be patient."

"I am not a patient man, Isabella. I need this girl looking presentable and ready to travel soon. I will give you the two weeks you ask for. That will have to be enough time. Do you understand?"

"I understand what you are telling me, Hernando, but do not ever try to threaten me. If not for my dead husband's former association with you, I would have nothing to do with you. I do not like what you do for your money. You must remember that the people associated with the people you work for know me very well. They respected what my husband and I did for them for several years. They are honest business people. They are not like you and the scum you have working for you."

Hernando silently grimaced when she mentioned her connections in Europe. He knew that many of the people behind the international drug smuggling ring he was currently involved with had no connection with the parent company.

Hernando's clandestine plan was to sell two or three girls to the Arabs, providing him with enough money to leave and move to Mexico. He would just disappear. No one would ever find him. He no longer loved his wife. She had given him no children. He was sure that he would find a younger woman, perhaps very young, who would readily marry him for his money.

His contact, the man who got him into the drug business, was actually unknown to the principles of the parent company. If they knew, they would quickly dispose of him and all of the people associated with him. Hernando recognized that he was on borrowed time. His responsibilities at the Guatemalan division of the company had long been ignored.

His leadership had produced very few contracts for his parent company's import-export business. Subsequently, very few profits were declared. His European superiors were not happy with the way things were going.

22

Mattie looked across the table at Charlene. The woman had a troubled look on her face.

"What's bothering you, Charlene? Are things not going as you planned?"

"Oh, I'm okay. I just was thinking about how everything will be when you three girls leave to go back to your families. You have no idea how much help you have been to me. The kids love all of you."

"Hey, we've only been here for a week. We still have almost two months to be with you. The girls and I are absolutely elated with being here. Working with the kids is such a rewarding experience. The teenagers are a little more difficult as they have been forced to grow up really fast.

"We're just getting settled and moved in. Don't start trying to worry about when we leave. Your friend, Marta, should be coming back to you just about the time we need to leave."

Alicia was listening to the exchange between Mattie and Charlene. She reached across the table and put her hand on top of Charlene's.

"Okay Sister Charlene, what have you got planned today for your fellow workers? Are we back into the schoolroom, or do we have cleaning assignments? I'm excited to get started. It's almost nine in the morning here, and we need you to point us to our duties."

Charlene looked across the table at the three girls and smiled. "I was thinking today that we might all go on a field trip. I would like to take the three of you

151

around the countryside. Maybe we can go into the city and have a nice lunch. I have a few dollars set aside."

"That's a great idea, but I need to tell you that you can't buy our lunch. My dad will. He gave me enough money to buy everyone in this village lunch. I think he was worried that I would starve," Mattie said. "I'm excited about the sightseeing excursion. We only got a few glimpses of the countryside and some of the city streets when Pablo drove us here from the airport. Will just the four of us be going?"

"Yes, I will leave Pablo here to look after the children. He will also fix their lunch. He helps me in the kitchen most of the time. Actually, I have found him to be a very creative cook. He has been able to take some very plain ingredients and turned them into a flavorful meal. The kids all like when he cooks.

"You cannot wear your shorts and your sleeveless tops like you have been around here when we head out. I was going to mention this to you, but I haven't had the opportunity. These people are very strict about how women dress on the streets. You can wear jeans like the ones you had on when you arrived. I know that it is very warm and very humid here, but those are the people's customs and we must respect them."

Alicia looked at the other two girls and responded, "That's okay with us. None of us brought much of a wardrobe anyway. Everything we have is in our backpacks. We didn't know about the customs here. We've been hot, and we wanted to be comfortable, but we will respect your wishes and stick with the local customs."

THE VILLA

All three girls agreed and went to their room to change into their jeans and T-shirts. All three were wearing the same T-shirt that had Multnomah School of the Bible emblazoned on both the front and back.

Bethany was the first one back into the dining area. Charlene was still sitting in her chair at the head of the table and was waiting for them to return. She looked up and smiled.

"Seeing all three of you dressed like that gives me butterflies. I really do miss all of the friends I made while I was at Multnomah. What a truly wonderful institution. You three are going to be the talk of the town. You look great in your matching T-shirts."

"Are you sure that this is okay? We can all change into something different if you think we should," Bethany said.

"You three look great. Don't change a thing. I will be very proud to show you off to our city."

Pablo was standing on the front stoop of the building smiling and waving as the four ladies climbed into the old van. Having heard that they planned to be using the van for a tour, he had cleaned out the inside and washed all of the windows. Then he washed the exterior. Despite all of the dents and scratches, the van looked pretty good.

Charlene climbed behind the wheel and started in the direction of their little town called Santa Inés. Then, she drove to the center of the town, which listed its population at less than ten thousand inhabitants. Charlene maneuvered the stretch van into a space in front of a big square that was about three blocks off the paved highway.

"This is our town square. I enjoy coming here in the evening sometimes. Just about everyone in town comes to the square late in the afternoon. Many of them stay here until well into the evening. They bring their children and their pets. You won't see many people during the day; only in the evenings do you see people congregate. The town also has a very old Catholic mission. Perhaps one day we will come and visit the mission.

"Get out of the van, and I will show you our marketplace. It is just down between those two buildings."

The marketplace was large in size and housed a few small cubicles that contained local produce as well as small pens of chickens and small hogs. The air was humid, and the smell was horrible. A few of the vendors were selling local arts, crafts, and other items more than likely produced by the residents of the area.

"This country has had traditions handed down for thousands of years. They have a broad diversity from the colorful clothing of the Maya in the highlands to the beach lifestyle of the Garinagu in the east. I have been told that Guatemala is the most culture-rich country in Latin America."

"Ladies, the landscape and geography of Guatemala is just as diverse as its people. With the highland mountain ranges to the low-lying costal areas, Guatemala is a hotbed of bio-diversity. Rainforests cover much of the lowlands while the mountains have a more arid environment. All kinds of vegetation and animal life can be found throughout the country.

"Although I have been here for nearly fifteen years, I haven't seen but a small portion of the country.

I have not been to the Mayan ruins that are near the coast to the east. Perhaps sometime in the future, you will have the opportunity to see more of the country. I only wish that I had the time and the resources to show you what I have been told exists just a few miles from the center of Guatemala City. Let's go back to our van, and I will take you into the city."

Charlene and the girls climbed back into the van. She turned, once again onto the paved portion of the road leading to Guatemala City. The drive took nearly an hour before they began to see the city materialize in front of them.

They saw many tall buildings. The city itself looked like any other major city throughout the world. It was only when you looked down the narrow streets and the dark alleyways that you realized that you were indeed in a third world country.

"We are very close to the center of the city. This is a good place to stop, as I see a parking space just ahead. We can walk to the restaurant that I wish to take you to. It is just a short distance away."

Charlene and the girls walked slowly down the street, occasionally stopping to look into the windows of the shops displaying a wide variety of goods.

Bethany stopped in front of a window and stared at the colorful dress displayed on the mannequin. It had brilliant colors and appeared to be almost full length.

"That is one of the styles that is common with the ladies in the highlands. If you look up into the hills, you will see some very high mountains that surround this city. The area has many small villages similar in size as our little village. In many cases, the people dress very differently than the inhabitants of the lowlands."

"That's our restaurant just ahead. I think you will enjoy this. It is always good to try the food of different cultures when you travel. I have become very used to their cuisine over the years."

The girls entered the small café that Charlene had chosen. She elected for them to take a table near the entrance so that they could see the people walking by.

When the waiter approached the table, Charlene spoke to him in fluent Spanish with a dialect common to the area. The girls understood most of what she said but had confused looks on their faces when the conversation reversed between the waiter and Charlene.

"I can tell by the looks on your faces that some of the dialogue didn't sound like the Spanish we all learned in school. Am I right?"

"You are absolutely right," Alicia said, "You lost me a couple of times. Honestly, I thought I was pretty good at speaking the language."

"You do well enough to get started. You'll soon learn their dialect."

Lunch was ordered and the three continued to chat about everything they had seen on their way into the city.

Mattie turned to Charlene and asked why the two men sitting in the corner booth were constantly staring at them.

"You are an oddity here. They are not used to seeing blonde ladies in Guatemala."

23

The men Mattie had referred to were none other than Hernando Banderas' two lieutenants. They had been sent to find exactly what they were seeing … three beautiful blonde women who looked within the age specifications that had been described to them.

Felipe looked at Garcia and then back to the girls sitting with Charlene. He turned back and spoke in a low voice.

"Amigo, those three blonde girls fit the description of the women Señor Banderas has told us to look for. What should we do?"

"We must wait until they finish their meal. Then, we will follow them to where they live."

"But we are supposed to return to the office when we are finished with our lunch, which is right about now. Señor Banderas will be furious."

"He will not be angry if we return with information that will help us catch the blonde girls that are sitting at that table. Do not worry. We must wait until they leave, and then we must be cautious to follow them so that they do not see us. Do you understand?"

"Yes, I understand. How should we do this?"

"When they are almost finished, we both leave. I will stay on this side of the street, and you will go to the other side. We must find where they are going. We must attempt to get the license number of their vehicle. If we get that information, then Señor Banderas will know where to find them again. If we follow them to a hotel, then we will know where they are staying. We must be cautious to follow them until we discover the information that we need."

"I agree, Felipe. We must not lose contact with these girls. If we are successful and we are able to capture these lovely ladies, then Señor Banderas will be very pleased. Then he will give us each the money he has promised."

The two men smiled at each other, considering the possibilities of providing their employer with the information he sought and also receiving a reward. They were thinking of the 1,000 quetzals that Señor Banderas had promised to pay for each girl that they brought to him.

* * *

The ladies took their time eating their lunch. When they had all finished, Mattie reached into the money belt that she had strapped to her waist and extracted several U.S. bills.

"They will take that money here, but you will lose quite a bit in the transaction. I believe that if you are going to want to spend money while you are here that you should convert some of your money to quetzals. You will find that 1 US dollar would equal approximately 7.60 Guatemalan quetzals. Let's go to the bank across the street and exchange some of your money now," Charlene advised.

"You know, I don't see where I will be spending much money while we are here. However, exchanging some of it would be a good idea. My dad, who thinks I should never be short of financial resources, gave me 1,000 US dollars and a new American Express credit card. I have it all in my money belt."

They were wide-eyed when she told them how much money she was carrying.

Bethany let out a gasp as she turned to stare at Mattie. "Can I get your daddy to adopt me?"

The room was filled with their laughter at Bethany's remark. They all agreed to walk across the street and exchange Mattie's 1,000 US dollars for nearly 7,600 Guatemalan quetzals.

Mattie made the comment that she wanted to divide the money up between the four of them, just in case they got separated or individually needed some money. Bethany and Alicia agreed that they would each take 1,000 quetzals. They also decided to place whatever amount Mattie did not want to carry with her in Charlene's safe at the mission.

When the girls had finished lunch and Mattie had paid the bill, they walked across the street to the Azteca Bank.

At the same time the girls had walked out of the restaurant, Felipe directed Garcia to a position not far from the bank. Then he rose and exited the restaurant. He walked slowly down his side of the street. He stopped when he saw the girls enter the bank. He stood at the corner and waited for about fifteen minutes. He could observe Garcia doing the same at the corner past the bank.

Felipe was beginning to wonder what had happened when he saw the four women leave the bank and walk in his direction. At the corner, they crossed over to his side and continued walking. He watched as they climbed into the old green van. He saw Garcia stop short of the corner and watch him. He kept on walking until he came up to the van.

"Buenos dias, ladies. I saw you having lunch at the same restaurant as my associate and I. Are you beautiful ladies visiting our city?"

Charlene said in English, "Don't answer him. I don't like when strangers ask questions."

The girls ignored the man as they had been directed and climbed into the van, hurriedly closed the doors, and locked them. Charlene started the car and quickly drove off. Felipe memorized the license number of the van. As soon as it was out of site, he wrote down the number on the back of an envelope he had in his shirt pocket.

He motioned for Garcia to join him. When Garcia arrived, he slapped his friend on the back and said, "Hey, Amigo, let us go into the cantina on the corner and have a drink to celebrate our discovery."

Garcia quickly agreed as the two of them walked to the corner and entered the cantina. They did not have just one beer; they had several. After nearly two hours, both men were staggering as they walked to their car. Felipe got behind the wheel.

"Felipe, do you think you are okay to drive? You are very drunk, amigo. Perhaps we should take a taxi to our office. If we get stopped by a policeman, we will both be in jail."

"You're right, Garcia. I will take a taxi with you. But first, let us rest here for a while. I am very sleepy."

The two men leaned back in the front seat of their Ford sedan and were quickly fast asleep.

They were sleeping soundly when they both woke up to a pounding on the car door. Standing just outside of the door were two uniformed policemen scowling at them through the closed window.

"Open the door, hombres. You are not allowed to park and sleep on our city streets. Let me see your driver's license. You have been parked here for well over an hour. Do you know that parking is restricted to one hour?"

The two men looked at each other in dismay. Finally, Felipe withdrew his driver's license and presented it to the policeman whom he had determined to be the senior officer.

"Felipe Escalante, where are you employed?"

"I am employed by Señor Hernando Banderas of the Consolidated International Trading Corporation. I am one of his assistants, as is my partner sitting next to me, Señor Garcia Marquez."

24

Mattie, Bethany, and Alicia were sitting at the breakfast table discussing their plans for the day. Charlene walked in, looked at the three girls, sat down, and joined them.

"I thought you girls said you were runners. I believed you would be out jogging around our little compound. I used to do that, but I think I just got lazy and figured I'd get enough exercise running around inside this building."

"You're right, Charlene. Alicia, Bethany, and I were just suggesting that we go for a run. As you said, we will not wear our normal running shorts. I think we have decided that we can each cut off the legs on one pair of our jeans. We really do miss our daily run around the campus. Is it okay for us to run on the road that leads into town?"

"I don't see a problem with either question. I hate to see you ruin a good pair of jeans, but I think that short-shorts are just a little too objectionable for our local society.

"I would stay on the main road, and I think the safest thing is for the three of you to run together. How long do you plan to be gone?"

"We usually run out for twenty minutes and then back for twenty minutes. A good estimate is that we will be gone for about forty-five minutes. Does that sound good?"

"That sounds just fine. When the three of you get back, we'll plan out the rest of our day. I thought maybe we could consider taking some of the kids on a field trip to see some of the ruins."

"Wow, we'd like to see that, too! How far is it to these ruins you are referring to? How long should we plan to be gone?"

"I need to check with Pablo to be sure that he will be here while we are gone. Going to the ruins is just a day trip. The Mixco Viejo Mayan ruins aren't nearly as magnificent as Tikal or Quirigua, but these ruins are a favored spot for day-trippers from Guatemala City.

"The ruins are dated back to the 12th century and are believed to be the remains of a ceremonial site. It is made up of many temples and a palace as well as several ball courts that were used to play the Mayan ballgame of pitziil, a game that is a mix of soccer and volleyball."

"Charlene, that really sounds like fun. We weren't sure that we would be able to see any of the sites while we were here. We didn't know what your schedules or plans might be. I know that Mattie and Alicia are just as excited as I am to see something that goes that far back in history."

"You gals get ready and go do your run. I'll make arrangements for us to take the trip. I can make us a lunch, and we can eat on the road. As soon as you return, we can leave."

The three girls took only a few minutes to cut the bottoms off the legs of their jeans. They all laughed at each other as soon as they saw what they looked like. They headed out the door and took to the road in front of the mission. They ran to the left side of the road so that they would be facing traffic, which is consistent with practice in the United States.

As they rounded a bend in the road a short distance from the Mission, they heard a car approaching behind them. They thought little of it. They just moved into single file, farther off the road on the opposite side.

When the car was beside them, it slowed down. Before the girls could see who was in the car or determine why the car had slowed down, the car sped off down the road toward Santa Inés.

"Who do you suppose that was?" Alicia asked as they continued down the road.

"I have no idea, but I am glad they drove off," Mattie said. "I felt like they were watching us, and that made me nervous. Hey, Bethany, you back there?"

For a brief moment, Mattie's heart stopped, worrying about her friend, until Bethany replied through her huffs and puffs, "Sorry, I'm back here. You two are setting the pace. I got a look at the car, but I couldn't see the people inside. I think maybe they don't see too many people running down the roads here in Guatemala."

The three girls continued their run toward the small town. Mattie looked at her watch and said that they needed to reverse directions and head back to the mission. None of the girls thought about the car that had slowed down and sped off. They made their turn, crossed to the opposite side of the road and headed back, never stopping or changing their pace.

They jogged back to the center of the mission compound. They ran up the stairs to their room, each grabbing a change of clothes, and headed down the long hallway to the bath facilities. They took turns using the shower. When all three had taken showers and dressed, they headed back to their room.

The smaller children playing in the courtyard below looked up, pointing at the three girls with big towels wrapped around their heads, and laughed. Mattie looked at her watch and commented that they had taken a full hour to do their run, shower, and come back downstairs.

Charlene was sitting in her office doing paperwork as she waited for her passengers. She got up from behind her desk and looked at the three girls as they entered. All three were standing in a row waiting for their leader to tell them what to do next.

"You three look like you enjoyed your run down the roads of Guatemala. Did you see any dangerous animals, spiders, or snakes?"

"You didn't tell us to look out for those creepy things," Bethany said. "You should have warned us! All we saw was a car slow down to gawk at us. We didn't see who was in the car since it sped off almost immediately."

"I didn't tell you because I thought that might spoil your run if you were constantly looking for something perilous. Every once in a while you may see a snake on the roadway or perhaps the occasional large spider, but very few animals. I wasn't worried. They don't like us any more than we like them. Pablo is constantly checking our grounds to make sure that none of those things enter the compound."

"I also must warn you about hoodlums; this area can be dangerous. I don't want to scare you, as I am sure your parents shared enough of the 'what could happen,' but while you are here, stay alert and stay together," Charlene offered.

"I have selected four little ones to accompany us on our trip to the Mixco Viejo Mayan ruins. None of these kids have ever been very far from this facility. This will be good for them to see some of the sites that are located in their native country. Pablo will stay here and look after the remaining kids. We will be back in ample time for you to taste some of his cooking. As I told you, he is really quite good at preparing his native cuisine."

* * *

The drive to the Mayan ruins took two hours. Although they were located only 50 kilometers from Guatemala City, they had to travel nearly 100 kilometers from the mission compound. The traffic was horrendous due to numerous slow-moving vehicles as well as donkey-drawn carts. Charlene proved to be a very cautious driver as she wove her way through the crowded streets of the city and the poorly paved highway.

When they arrived at the ruins, Charlene commented that she saw a tour bus loading passengers. With very few other vehicles in the parking area, the ruins would not be crowded.

Charlene had been to the site previously and provided the girls with a full rundown. She spoke quietly yet professionally. She emphasized some of the Mayan words in order for the girls to understand not only the language but also the culture.

"Ladies, Mixco was the capital of the Pocomam Mayan Kingdom and was sometimes known as

Pocomam and Saqik'ajol Nimakaqapek in addition to Mixco."

"The original site was founded on a mountain top in the 12th century. They say the population in the early 16th century was around 10,000 people. Subsequently, they were conquered by Spanish conquistadors in the 1500s. As the story goes, the conquistadors then had the city burnt and the population forced out."

They toured the ruins for nearly an hour before Charlene suggested that they head back to the mission. Pablo would be well into the preparation of the evening meal. She told the girls that he was excited about having the opportunity to impress the girls with his culinary expertise.

Although they had eaten a large lunch on the way to the ruins, they were looking forward to Pablo's evening meal. They speculated as to what he would be preparing. Alicia leaned back in her seat and commented that, whatever it was, she didn't want to know the ingredients until *after* she had eaten.

The drive back to the mission was much like the drive to the ruins. The traffic was heavy with constant horns honking. The trip included a lot of stopping and starting as the road was filled with carts and occasionally a farmer herding his animals down the middle of the right-of-way.

Charlene was continuously talking, commenting on various sites and points of interest.

"I think I could drive you three around this city for hours, and we would never come close to seeing all of the points of interest. I cannot imagine that this area was heavily populated long before our country was even discovered."

The four little ones that Charlene had selected to join them on their trip to the ruins had sat quietly for almost the entire trip. They didn't comment on any of the sites that Charlene had pointed out.

One small six-year-old boy had been especially quiet and had not uttered a word since they had left. Now as they were nearing the mission, he leaned forward and tapped Alicia on the shoulder. He spoke with a soft voice that was almost impossible to hear. Only Alicia and Bethany heard his inquiring words.

"I heard you talking about Jesus. I know about Jesus. I have listened to Sister Charlene tell us about Jesus. You said you had Jesus living in your heart. Can He come and live in my heart, too?"

Alicia turned in her seat so that she could face the small boy. He had a look on his face that almost brought tears to her eyes. He could not see Bethany, but she truly *did* have tears streaking down her face.

"They told me your name is Mathew. Did you know that Mathew was one of Jesus' disciples? When we get back home and after dinner, I will tell you how you can have Jesus living in your heart, too. Would you like that?"

The young boy was still leaning forward and quickly nodded his head and then leaned back in his seat.

Charlene parked the van in its usual spot and proceeded to help the little ones as they crawled to the open door. As soon as their feet hit the ground, they all ran to the building's front entrance.

Alicia noticed Bethany was wiping tears from her face and reached out and gave her a hug.

"God is good, isn't He?" Alicia said, inspired.

Bethany nodded her head, turned to Mattie, who was getting out of the front seat of the van, walked over, and whispered, "Our friend, Alicia, has made a hit with that little guy called Mathew. They're going to talk about Jesus after dinner."

Mattie turned and watched as Alicia approached. She spread her arms, motioning for a hug, and said, "God has decided to put you in the game, Sister Alicia. Don't drop the ball!"

As they entered the building, they could smell the tantalizing odor of food cooking. Pablo was busy in the kitchen preparing the evening meal, and the smells were unusual in that they did not remind the girls of any of the food that had been prepared by Charlene.

"I think we're all going to experience authentic Guatemalan cuisine," Mattie said. "I don't know about you, Alicia, but Bethany and I are going to pork out on whatever Pablo has cooking. It smells delicious."

Pablo was preparing traditional foods based on Mayan cuisine. The food featured corn, chilies, and beans as key ingredients. He also prepared enchiladas and quesadillas unlike anything their Mexican counterparts make in the states.

He told the girls that if he prepared dinner for them again, he would prepare paches, a kind of tamale made from potatoes. Pablo pointed out that paches were generally eaten only on Thursday while on Saturday they usually prepared traditional tamales. He added that they were a tradition during the Christmas holidays.

25

Hernando's office was filled with the pungent smell of cigar smoke. The two men walking through the door had difficulty seeing to the other end of the giant office. Señor Hernando Banderas was sitting, slouched down behind the desk, continually puffing on the large Cuban cigar wedged between his yellow, stained teeth.

"Tell me, did you find where the three girls are living?"

"Si, Señor Banderas. We have found that they are staying at that orphanage that you told us about. We followed them, and we know exactly where to grab them. We have watched this orphanage now for three days."

"Do you have a plan to get them for me? When can you get them?"

"We will need for you to obtain a taser gun for us. We have studied the effects of using these taser guns, and we believe that we can stun the girls while they are running down the road."

"What do you mean, 'running down the road'?"

"What we mean, Señor Banderas, is that they have been observed every day running beside the road leading from that orphanage toward the village of Santa Inés. We have observed them while they run for nearly an hour. They run toward the village for twenty minutes, and then they turn around and run back to the orphanage. We understand that it is an American custom."

"Tell me about your plan."

"Our plan is for you to provide us with a van so that we can capture all three girls. We plan to drive the van slowly alongside of the running girls. When we get into position, Garcia will taser them and stun each girl. We will put them into the back of the van and drive them to Señora Coronado's plantation. She will keep all of the girls until you are ready to sell them to the Arabs."

"When do you plan to catch these girls for me?"

"We are planning to get them tomorrow when they are running back from Santa Inés. We believe that they all will be very tired and will not put up any struggle."

"This sounds like a good plan. I am not sure that it will be as easy as you say. I am going to send Diego, my man from Florida, with you. He is the one that brought us the girl that is now staying with Señora Coronado. He has experience with this sort of thing."

"I will have the van for you today. I will contact the people in Belize and tell them that we will have four chickens for their little coop. Be back here at eight o'clock tonight. Meet me in the parking garage downstairs, do you understand?"

"Si, Señor Banderas. We will do exactly as you say. We will capture the girls and take them directly to Señora Coronado's plantation."

"You must not fail. I am depending on both of you."

Felipe and Garcia left the office and headed straight to a cantina. Felipe said to Garcia, "Tomorrow we will be rich. Let us celebrate with a few Corona beers before we pick up the van."

THE VILLA

* * *

Hernando Banderas leaned back in his chair and lit another cigar. He blew smoke rings into the air as he thought of what he would do when he was paid.

His plans were to demand that the Arab sheiks pay him in coins. They would be easy to convert to cash anywhere in the world. The coins could not be traced. He had checked on the value and discovered that each Austrian Philharmonic gold coin was trading at nearly 2,000 US dollars.

He would demand 400 of these gold coins for the four girls. He knew he would have to negotiate, and he would settle for 200 coins. This would provide him with $400,000. He calculated that he could carry the 200 coins in his briefcase.

Hernando had talked to the pilot of the airplane that he chartered to pick up the girl in Florida. He stated that he could arrange for an airplane that would fly him to anywhere in Mexico. The cost to Hernando would be 20,000 US dollars.

His strategy would be for him to walk away from his life in Guatemala. He certainly had no love for his wife of twenty years. Hernando had no intention of taking anyone with him. He would not consider any of the women he had been seeing for the past two years. He would start a new life.

He knew that he would need at least four days to complete the arrangements with the Arabs. He ground out his cigar, stood up, and headed for the door. He was reaching for the doorknob when it suddenly opened.

"Señor Banderas, I want to tell you that I can no longer work for you as your secretary or as your receptionist," the dark-haired young woman suddenly was saying. "I know now what you are doing, and I believe it is a great sin to sell drugs to people. It will destroy their lives. I am a Christian, and I cannot be a part of this company anymore. I wish to tell you that even though I do not have another job, I will be leaving at the end of the week."

Hernando stared at the beautiful young lady that stood before him. He saw tears streaming down her face.

"I think you are mistaken about what we do here. We are an import-export company. We ship and receive goods from all over the world. Who has told you these lies?"

"They are not lies. I know the truth. I want to work for four more days, and then I want to leave this horrid place forever."

"As you wish, Señorita. You will have a job here until the end of the week. Then you can leave."

* * *

The sun had gone down, and the streetlights of Guatemala City were glowing as Felipe and Garcia walked out of the cantina. Felipe looked at his watch and saw that the time was nearly eight o'clock. He had no intention of being late to meet Señor Banderas in the parking garage below the Hernandez building. They had consumed only three beers while they waited for evening. He felt very sober. He looked at his partner and determined that he, too, was not drunk.

When they entered the parking garage of the Hernandez building, they saw Señor Banderas standing beside a black van talking to the man they knew only by the name Diego. He was the man that brought in the blonde girl staying with Señora Coronado. They stopped a few feet from the van.

"Good evening, Señor Banderas. We are here as you directed. Is this the van we shall use to pick up the young girls?"

"Yes, this is the van you will use. What time will you start from here? Señor Diego will be joining you. He will assist you to get the girls in the van."

"Garcia and I have decided to stay with the van tonight. We will leave at five in the morning before daylight. We'll drive an hour to the place where we can be in a position near the orphanage. We usually see the girls running at seven in the morning."

"Excellent. Diego will be here in the garage at exactly five in the morning. Can you do that, Diego?"

"Si, Señor Banderas. My hotel is only a few blocks from this building. I will be here at five in the morning."

* * *

Mattie, Alicia, and Bethany jogged out the main entrance to the orphanage at their usual time on a cloudy Monday morning. Mattie looked at her watch and saw that it was just a few minutes past seven.

The girls were delighted with the overcast skies as the air in this part of Guatemala was always thick and humid. They knew from experience that if the sun came out, temperatures became almost unbearable to run. Several times they had returned soaking wet from perspiration.

They had all become very accustomed to their route. They had now been in Guatemala for three weeks. The surrounding area was beginning to be familiar.

Without speaking, they formed a single file and started their run. Mattie was bringing up the rear this time.

They had made their turn and were on their way back when Mattie heard an approaching car. She paid no attention to the car coming from behind her.

As the van neared, Garcia was sitting on the floor with his feet hanging out of the side door, pointing a taser at Mattie's back. When he was alongside of her, he pulled the trigger. Mattie heard a loud crack and then let out a scream. The van stopped, and he jumped toward her prone body and quickly picked her up. He literally threw her to Diego, who was crouching beside the open door.

Garcia turned and began the chase to catch up with the other two girls. They had seen what had just happened and were running as fast as they could down the road.

Both girls were screaming at the top of their lungs as they entered the center courtyard. "Help! We need help!"

Charlene came out of the kitchen at a dead run.

"What? What? What?" she screamed at the two girls. "Where is Mattie?"

The girls struggled to catch their breaths and were sobbing as they explained what had just happened.

"Did you see the man? Did you get the license number? What kind of a car was it?"

"It was a black van. We didn't look back. We don't know the make and didn't get the license number."

26

At six o'clock in the morning, the phone rang in the kitchen. Dan was leaning against the kitchen counter watching Jessie prepare breakfast and walked over to the phone, picking up the receiver.

"Hello, this is Dan Branson."

The voice on the other end sounded hysterical, and he had difficulty understanding the person calling. Charlene was weeping uncontrollably and could not talk. Alicia took over the receiver.

"Mr. Branson, this is Alicia."

Dan could hear her suck in her breath before she started to talk again.

"Mattie has been kidnapped. It just happened about fifteen minutes ago while we were doing our morning run. I just got off the phone with the police."

The blood was literally draining from Dan's face. He could barely stay on his feet. He clenched his fist and his teeth.

"I'm on my way. I'll get Mattie back from those scumbags."

Jessie had her hand over her mouth and was moaning, "No, no, no, please tell me, no!"

Dan grabbed Jessie and brought her to him. She was shaking all over, moaning and sobbing at the same time.

"They got our girl, Jessie. Some devils down there have our girl. Please help me get packed. I need to go. I need to go now."

Danny had no idea what was taking place at the ranch house. He was busily feeding the horses when he turned and saw his dad literally running towards the Suburban. His mom was right behind him. He dropped his bucket and ran to the house. As he rounded the corner of the house, all he could see was the dust left behind by the Suburban racing out of the driveway.

Dan and Jessie were speeding up the highway toward the Redmond Airport. Jessie, no longer weeping, although still shaking, looked over to Dan.

"Slow down, Dan. We can't help Mattie if we both end up in the hospital. You're doing 85. I'll pray while you drive."

Dan looked in the rearview mirror and saw red lights flashing from a sheriff's car. He pounded the steering wheel and slammed on the brakes. Before the Suburban had come to a full stop, he crammed the shift into park and jumped out. He ran to the door of the deputy's car, now with the window open, and peered in. Fortunately, he knew the young deputy.

"Ernie, I have got to get to the airport. Somebody has kidnapped my daughter."

Dan didn't wait for a comment. He turned on his heel, ran back to the Suburban, and rammed the gearshift into drive. As he pulled out, the deputy sped by him with his siren blaring.

Dan drove into the parking area of the airport and dashed for his plane. He had called on his way and asked them to tow his plane out, do a preflight inspection for him, and provide him with WAC charts all the way to Central America. He said this was an emergency and asked them to hurry.

Doug, the young man manning the gas pumps, handed Dan the charts he had requested as he was climbing into the cockpit of his Cessna 310.

Jessie watched as Dan taxied out and took off in a southerly direction. She turned and saw Bob Simpson walking up to her. He pulled her to him.

"I know I shouldn't tell you to relax, but I need to. That guy of yours will get your daughter back for you. I have never known a guy who has such strength and fortitude as Dan."

Jessie held her head against Bob's chest and began to weep again. She didn't want to cry anymore, but she just couldn't hold it back.

"I know you're right, Bob. I just can't bare the thought of Mattie being in the hands of those devils, whoever they are. I know she's tough, but she is *my* precious daughter and gift from God."

"I put in a call to Ed Harris in DC," Bob said. "He's with the CIA now. I got lucky and got right through to him. I told him I didn't know any of details, but that Dan was flying his own plane to Guatemala. Jessie, do you know if he thought about grabbing his passport?"

"I don't think so. With the way he packed, he will be wearing pretty much the same clothing until he gets back home … *if* he gets back."

Jessie's cell phone rang.

"Mom, this is Danny. What's going on? Where are you? Where's Dad?"

"I'll be home in a few minutes, and I'll tell you everything."

* * *

Dan contacted the Redmond Flight Service and filed an instrument flight plan to Albuquerque, New Mexico. He calculated that it was exactly 982 air miles. He climbed to his assigned altitude of 11,000 feet and took up a heading direct to Albuquerque. The winds aloft were reported at ten knots, right on his tail.

He ran the numbers several times and determined that if he maintained his ground speed at 200 MPH he would arrive in Albuquerque in close to five hours. He had left Redmond at a quarter to seven, just forty-five minutes from the time he received Alicia's call. Albuquerque was on Mountain Time, an hour later. This meant he would land around one in the afternoon local time.

His fuel tanks all indicated full, which provided him with 150 gallons of fuel—fifty gallons in each of the tip tanks and another twenty-five gallons in each of the auxiliary tanks. He leaned his fuel flow to each engine and brought his exhaust gas temperatures to just below peak. He calculated that the two engines would burn twenty-five gallons per hour. That meant he would have approximately twenty-five gallons, give or take a couple of gallons, when he landed in Albuquerque. *Plenty of fuel*, he thought.

"If the winds don't change, I won't need to stop," he said out loud, even though no one was around to hear.

He had flown for nearly an hour in clear blue skies, maintaining his ground speed he calculated to be right at 206 MPH. He was drawn from studying his charts when he heard his transmitter calling him.

"Twin Cessna triple-three-delta-bravo. This is Salt Lake Center, do you copy?"

"Roger, Salt Lake, this is triple-three-delta-bravo."

"Triple-three-delta-bravo, we've been directed to have you contact a U.S. military channel on 131.25. Do you copy?"

"Roger, Salt Lake. Changing frequencies now. I'll come back to you later."

"Military radio, this is twin Cessna triple-three-delta-bravo, do you copy?

"Twin Cessna triple-three-delta-bravo, stand by one."

Suddenly, Dan heard a familiar voice. "Hey, Danny Boy. Ed Harris here with the 'you-know-who' company. I understand you're on your way to Guatemala City. I just talked to Jessie, and she said you went off without your passport. How did you plan to get through customs? I guess I should go ahead and tell you that I talked to the people across town. They will have a duplicate waiting for you when you arrive at Guatemala City.

"Additionally, if you're interested, a company jet carrying DEA people, a Gulfstream Four, will be sitting at the Air National Guard hangar on the Albuquerque Airport. If you think you can handle just being a passenger, I can get you a hop to where you are going. They won't leave until five this evening. It'll get you there faster. What do you think?"

"I think that I am going to try and get you sainted. Ed, how did you pull this off?"

"You got a lot of people who like you, Danny Boy. Look for a blue station wagon when you land in Albuquerque. You'll recognize the markings. And by the way, good luck. Everybody here will be pulling for you."

"I have to ask. How do you manage to get into the aviation frequencies? You blew me away when I heard your voice coming over my aircraft transmitter.

"Well, Dan, you're actually talking to me through a satellite. This new job of mine has put a lot of fancy equipment at my disposal. When I heard what had happened, I pushed a few buttons, and here I am. Hey, cowboy, I have to run. Remember, you got friends rooting for you. I also know you'll be getting help from up above, too."

* * *

"Salt Lake Center, this is twin Cessna triple-three-delta-bravo back with you on 119.7

"Roger, triple-three-delta-bravo, radar contact, maintain 11,000."

"Roger, Salt Lake, triple-three-delta-bravo."

Dan's flight to Albuquerque was calculated perfectly. He looked at his watch as he was taxiing to the general aviation parking area and noted that he had missed his estimated time of arrival by only ten minutes. He looked at his fuel gauges and saw that he had also computed his fuel consumption correctly.

As he was anxiously standing by his plane watching the fuel truck top off all four of his fuel cells with 100-octane aviation fuel, a blue station wagon with Air Force markings and an orange checkered flag attached to the back drove up beside his plane.

"Are you Dan Branson?" the driver asked.

"That would be me. Are you my ride?"

"Yes, sir. The people over at Ops are expecting you. They said you could taxi your plane over to the other side of the field and leave it in our hangar."

"That would be great. Lead the way."

THE VILLA

The gas attendant required only a minute to complete the transaction and give Dan a receipt and a salute, indicating he was free to leave.

Dan climbed back into his plane, fired up the engines, and then followed the station wagon down the taxiway to the opposite side of the field. The sign above the large hangar door read New Mexico Air National Guard.

27

Mattie lay on the floor in the back of the van. The swaying of the van began to bring her back to consciousness. The man known as Diego looked down at her as she began to move her arms and legs.

"From where we are now, we will arrive at Señora Coronado's plantation in another hour. I am going to give her a small dose of Seconal. This will keep her asleep for at least two hours. It's not a dangerous drug, and she should not feel after-effects when she wakes up."

The van made its way down numerous paved and unpaved roads until it finally arrived at the half-mile long drive with a massive stone arch, indicating the entrance to the Villa de las Flores plantation.

Felipe had called Señora Coronado when they entered the plantation. She was standing on the steps leading into the massive three-story villa.

When they stopped, Diego opened the sliding door on the side of the van. Mattie, still unconscious, was lying on her back with her eyes closed. She did not move as Diego lifted her and carried her up the steps and through the entrance to the villa. Isabella Coronado motioned for him to follow her as she led him to a gated opening that turned out to be the entrance to an elevator. Once inside, she pushed a button and the ancient elevator began to move toward the upper floors.

The elevator stopped on the third floor. Isabella motioned once again for Diego to follow her as she led him into a very large bedroom, an exact duplicate of the room where they had taken Amy. She pointed at the huge king-sized bed in the center of the room. Diego placed Mattie in the middle of the bed and then backed away.

"Leave. Leave now. I believe I know what you and your patron are doing. I do not approve of this. Tell Señor Banderas that I say he is a wicked man, and God will surely punish him for these evil deeds. Get out of my home. Use the stairs. Now leave!"

Felipe, who had followed them to the room, motioned for Diego to follow him. They went to the winding staircase that led to the main floor and hurried to their van, which was still waiting, idling at the front of the villa.

* * *

Mattie began to move as she slowly regained consciousness. When she opened her eyes, she observed Isabella smiling, sitting on the edge of her bed.

She looked around the spacious, elegantly furnished room and then turned her attention to Isabella.

"Who are you? Where am I? Why was I kidnapped? What are you going to do with me?"

"I must start by introducing myself. I am Señora Isabella Coronado. This is my home. You are on my plantation, called Villa de las Flores. That name is translated to— "

"I know what it is translated to; I understand and speak Spanish," Mattie said angrily. "I will ask again. *Why* was I kidnapped? What are you planning to do with me?"

"I am trying to explain that to you. You are going to stay here with me at my home until they ship you away."

"Ship me away? What do you mean 'ship me away'? Who is that standing in the doorway? Is she one of your accomplices?"

Amy walked into the room. She had been leaning against the door jamb, listening to the interactions between Isabella and Mattie.

"You got it, sister. They're planning to literally ship you and me out. They plan to sell us to some Arab sheik that'll put us in his harem. I'm just like you. They snatched me off the street in Fort Lauderdale, Florida. They drugged me, and the next thing I saw was Isabella looking at me, the same way she is looking at you. By the way, she is not one of them. She may be the only hope we have."

"Who are 'they' that you keep referring to? Are they part of a ring of kidnappers? Is this something that they have done before?"

"Let's get some introductions going. You already know that I am Señora Isabella Coronado. This young lady is Amy Creston. She has already told you what has happened to her. What is your name? Where are you from? And, what brings you to Guatemala?"

"My name is Mattie Branson. I live with my family on a cattle ranch in Central Oregon. I am in Guatemala helping a missionary lady, Charlene Pearson, who operates an orphanage and a women's refuge near a little town by the name of Santa Inés. I am a student at a Bible college in Portland, Oregon. I volunteered along with two of my friends to work with Charlene for two months."

Isabella stood up from her seat on the end of the bed. Mattie, who was now sitting cross-legged in the middle of the bed, watched as Isabella moved in front of her. She lifted Mattie's arm and then examined the rest of her body that was mostly exposed as she wore only the short-sleeved top and cut-off jeans she had put on for running.

"You're pretty badly bruised up. How did all of this happen?" she asked Mattie as she lifted the back of her blouse.

"I think they zapped me with some kind of a stun gun. I don't really know. All I know was that I had fallen to the ground, and the next thing I saw was you staring at me lying on this bed."

"Well, you showed up in better condition than Amy. Despite all of your scrapes and bruises, you don't appear to be addicted to narcotics. Amy has had a tough time shedding the habit, but she has made it."

"You look like you could use a bath and some clean clothes. I'll let Amy show you where everything is. Your room is identical to hers. As a matter of fact, you both share the same bath facilities. Her room is just down the hall."

Isabella walked out of the room. She said she would be back in a few minutes and would lay a clean outfit on Mattie's bed. She had previously told Amy that she never threw anything away and most of the clothing she was providing the girls was garments that she had worn when she was younger.

Amy led Mattie into the huge bathroom with the giant sunken tub in the middle of the room. Mattie was still shaking and very nervous, but spoke to Amy. "I have to say, this is like in the movies. Have you used this yet? This room looks like it was designed after a world-class spa."

"You bet. I have used it just about every day. I had a pretty tough time shaking the drug habit. I had a friend . . . well, I guess I shouldn't call him a friend, introduce me to crack cocaine. I am rid of it now, but it took its toll on me. I don't ever want to go back there."

"Tell me about yourself, Amy. Where's your family? Are they looking for you?"

"Hardly. I went down to Florida for Spring Break two years ago. My family lives in Ohio, and I am an only child. I was a sophomore at Ohio State. Actually, I had pretty good grades and was maintaining a 3.2 GPA. I felt pretty good about myself.

"When I got hooked on crack, I called my folks and asked them for help. My dad was furious. He said that I was ruining the family name. He is big in our city. He said I should get lost and forget about home. I haven't been able to talk to them since. I tried to call my mom, but he won't let her talk to me."

"Amy, I'm sorry. That had to really hurt. I've been so blessed with a close, loving family. I need to excuse myself and head to the bathroom. This entire ordeal has been stressful, to say the least. Let's talk again."

Mattie excused herself and went back into the bathroom where she soaked for at least 30 minutes before she returned to the bedroom and found a complete set of clothes lying on her bed. She stood for a moment with a giant bath sheet wrapped around her body, thinking about where she was and what was happening to her.

"Hey, Mattie, get dressed and then come pound on my door. It is just on the other side of the bathroom we share. I'll take you around and show you the place. This giant villa and the plantation are unbelievable. I think Isabella is fixing us some lunch. She is a fantastic cook. I would gain 100 pounds if I stayed here very long."

Mattie quickly dressed in the clothes that Isabella had placed on the foot of her bed. Amazingly, everything fit perfectly. As she thought about Isabella, she recognized that she and Amy were about the same size. Obviously, Isabella had been about the same size as the two girls during her younger years.

Mattie knocked on Amy's door. She responded immediately, and the two walked through the large home, inspecting nearly every room. Isabella's room was identical, perhaps a little larger, to the ones that the girls occupied. All three of the monstrous bedrooms were located on the third floor of the villa.

The second floor had six more very large bedrooms. Each bedroom was tastefully furnished with three separate bathrooms strategically located between the bedrooms.

The main floor of the house included a library that was loaded floor to ceiling with mostly very old books. A glass-encased parlor faced the back patio with a high ceiling and large French doors that served as the entrance to the spacious gardens.

All of the rooms were very large, including a gigantic living room with an equally large fireplace. The dining room appeared as though you could easily seat fifty people. They discovered that fireplaces were in virtually every downstairs room. The bedrooms on the third floor each boasted their own marble fireplace.

Mattie and Amy entered the large kitchen and saw that Isabella was busily dishing lunch onto three gold-gilded plates.

"Sit down, ladies. I have prepared a small lunch for us. Tonight, I will have our cook prepare something very special. It will be my favorite."

28

A tall man wearing an Air Force flight-suit approached Dan, who noted that the man was probably six-foot-six and stood well above his own six-foot-two frame.

"Hi. We've been expecting you. I'm Major Steve Treadwell. I understand you made the trip from Oregon without a stop. Is that correct?"

Dan shook the man's hand and nodded his head in agreement with the major's statement.

"You're right about the nonstop flight. As you can well appreciate, I sure would like to use your facilities. Can you point me in the right direction? I'll chat with you after I take care of an urgent need," Dan said anxiously.

The major pointed to a door near the back of the hangar and gave Dan a big smile.

"I'll bet you set a record. You probably didn't drink any coffee this morning like I did."

Dan walked to the back of the hangar to the door the major had indicated. A few minutes later, he returned to the major, still standing beside Dan's aircraft.

"You have a beautiful bird here, Branson. She looks brand new. Do you fly her much?"

"As much as I possibly can. I'm a nut for flying. You probably already know this, but our Uncle taught me how to fly."

"As a matter of fact, I do know that. I read your file while I was waiting for you to get here. I saw that you got some time in KC135's over the gulf."

The two men chatted for a few minutes. Finally, the major walked over to the air-stair door leading up to the entrance into the Gulfstream. He motioned for Dan to follow him as he entered the main cabin and pointed to the second row of seats.

"That's going to be your seat all the way to Guatemala City. I'm going to be flying the left seat. Come up and tap Jerry, my copilot, on the shoulder, and he'll let you ride the right seat. That is if you feel like it.

"We're figuring a little over four hours in flight. I know that you are carrying a heavy burden. Don't hesitate to call on me if you need anything."

"Thanks, Steve. I just may do that. Can you tell me anything about my fellow passengers?"

"Yes, they are all DEA people. I understand that they just had a high-level meeting here in Albuquerque. My understanding is that drug traffic from Mexico and Central America are driving these people nuts. The Colombians have people everywhere now. We leave at five, but I prefer everyone be here at four-thirty."

* * *

At exactly four-thirty, Dan walked back into the big hangar and stood beside his plane. He had caught a ride over to the main terminal building, had a good lunch, and spent about fifteen minutes on his cell phone talking to Jessie. She told him that she had explained everything to Danny and that he had been very quiet ever since.

Dan saw four men and one woman walking into the hangar, moving toward the Gulfstream. They had all been briefed on his presence, and each of them came up to him and expressed their concern as well as their willingness to assist him if he should need them.

Steve Treadwell approached the plane and motioned for everyone to board the aircraft and take their assigned seats. Dan was seated next to the woman, who was stationed in D.C.

She stated that she was with the group primarily to keep records of everything that transpired. She smiled at him and said, "I'm a G12. That means that on this trip, I'm a glorified secretary. I don't have any family, I'm single, and I like to travel. I volunteered when I heard they needed someone to take notes."

The takeoff was smooth, as was the air at altitude. Dan looked at his watch and noted that they had departed about five minutes ahead of schedule. This meant that they would be landing in Guatemala City at about ten in the evening.

The woman picked up a magazine as Dan reclined in his seat to take a nap. He felt like he had only been asleep for a few minutes when he felt the aircraft touch down. He looked at his watch and noted the time was five after eight in the evening at the ranch. As the plane taxied to a small ramp opposite Guatemala City's main air terminal, Dan grabbed his old Air Force B-4 bag and prepared to exit the aircraft.

Two black GMC Suburbans pulled up alongside the aircraft. Dan was the last one off the aircraft and was surprised when a man who appeared to be about forty approached him and stuck out his hand.

"Hi, Dan. I'm Randy Johnson. We talked on the phone. Ed Harris gave me a call and said you would be coming in on one of our planes carrying the DEA people. How was the flight?"

"The flight was fine. I left Oregon at seven this morning, and here I am in Guatemala City. It's only eight in the evening at home. As you know, except for Ed's intervention, I would still be bouncing along, struggling my way through airports and political bureaucracy in Mexico. I didn't expect to get here for three days."

"Those folks all have their own ride," Randy said. "The other Suburban is mine for just the two of us. I got you a room with a king-size bed at the Barceló Hotel in the center of the city. It will be a good place from which to work. Besides that, the rates are reasonable."

"Ed told me to give you whatever assistance I can without getting involved with the locals. Here is your duplicate passport. I understand you went off in a hurry and didn't bring yours. We have to stop at the white building over there so you can clear customs and immigration."

The stop at the customs and immigration building took less than ten minutes. Actually, he and Randy had arrived before the DEA people. The officials were standing at their stations waiting for them to enter the room.

"What are your plans of action, Dan?" Randy asked.

"I've had several hours to think about what to do first. If possible, I believe I would like to record a personal message to go on television. What do you think?"

"Well, I have to tell you that the kidnapping was reported by the police; however, it got only a two-second spot on our local news at noontime. Your idea may be viable, but I have no idea what you would have to pay."

"The cost doesn't make any difference. I would like to have a thirty-second spot presented every thirty minutes all of tomorrow until midnight. Will that be possible?"

"I know the manager of the station. I don't know how receptive he would be to your request. Sometimes they don't care about the money or the issue. They like to do things their way, and that's it.

"I'll drop you at your hotel, and then I'll meet you for breakfast downstairs at seven in the morning."

"Randy, that would be great. I appreciate all of the help you and your people are giving me."

Dan checked into his room and set his bag down. He opened his bag and extracted an Iridium Satellite telephone. He flipped open the phone cover and found that he had a signal. He knew that his satellite phone would work anywhere in the world. He dialed the U.S. country code and his home phone number.

"Hello, this is Jessie Branson."

"Hello, Jessie, this is me. I'm in my room in Guatemala City. You would not believe all the help that Ed Harris' people are giving me. I can't believe that I made it down here as fast as I did. I left our plane in Albuquerque. I caught a hop on a government jet that got me into town about thirty minutes ago.

"Tomorrow morning Randy Johnson, one of Ed's people, will take me down to the TV station. I am going to try to make a recording and blast it on the local TV every 30 minutes all of tomorrow and tomorrow evening. I don't care what it costs. I will make it happen. Are you doing OK?"

"We're alright, Dan. Just be careful. What are you going to say in your recording?"

"I am going to tell these guys that I will meet their demands. I want our daughter back."

"I love you so much, Dan. Please call me often. I can't stand being here not knowing what is happening."

"I have my Iridium phone. I grabbed it out of my top drawer when I was packing. I forgot my passport but, again, Ed had a replacement waiting for me here in Guatemala City. The U.S. has a consulate here and was advised in advance that I would need a replacement passport in order to clear customs. They took care of everything. I'll call you as soon as I have something to report. Get some sleep. I love you, too."

Dan climbed into bed and stared at the ceiling of his hotel room. He had trouble believing that he was probably only a few miles from where his daughter was being held captive.

He tossed and turned for more than an hour before he finally drifted off into troubled sleep. He couldn't keep his mind off the horrible events that had taken place.

An hour later, he awoke abruptly. He got out of bed and knelt. His prayer was lengthy, interrupted several times by his sobs, yet he knew his plea had made it to the altar of God.

29

Felipe felt chills run through his body as he faced Hernando Banderas.

"We were able to capture only one of the three girls. We have taken her to Señora Coronado's plantation."

"I was told I would have three girls, not just one. Why have you failed me? When will you have the other two girls?"

"I do not believe we will be able to capture the other two girls. The police have been to the orphanage several times. They are looking for us at this very moment."

"I have been in contact with your man in Belize. He has told me that the Arabs will pay me only 300,000 quetzals for each girl. That would mean that it would equal only 80,000 US dollars."

"Señor Banderas, unless Garcia and I can find more young women who meet the Arab's requirements, I don't think we can do anything else."

"Get out of my office, both of you! You have failed me. I will call you if I need you. Until then, stay away from me. Do not come back here unless I call you."

"But, Señor, you have promised to pay us 1,000 quetzals for each girl. We captured a girl for you and took her to Señora Coronado's plantation. She is there now. When will Garcia and I receive our payment?"

"I said for you to get out of my office. I will not pay you for failing me. If I change my mind, I will call you. Now get out! I do not want to see you again. Do you understand?"

Felipe and Garcia turned and left the office. Hernando picked up the phone on his desk and dialed the number he had been given.

"Hello, this is Jose Corolla. Who is this calling?"

"This is Hernando Banderas. My man, Felipe, has talked to you. I am his employer. I have two females here for you. When can I expect you to come here and pick them up?"

"I was told that you would have four women. Am I wrong?"

"We are only able to provide two at this time. Again, I ask you, when can I expect you to come here for these two?"

"Do you understand that I told Felipe that I will pay only 300,000 quetzals for each woman?"

"Yes, I understand. When will you be here to take them away?"

"I will contact my people in Africa probably not before Friday of this week. I believe I can arrange to have them picked up then."

"That will be satisfactory. Do you and your people in Africa understand that I will be paid only in Austrian gold coins?"

"I will tell them. That should not be a problem. Call me on Thursday. Then I will be able to give you an exact time to have the girls at your airport."

Hernando did not have a chance to ask any further questions. He heard a click as Jose Corolla hung up the phone.

He spun around in his chair and reached for the remote for the television mounted on the wall behind his desk. Watching the news each morning was his custom. He had now been watching for news about the missing girl from the orphanage. He had heard only one brief report, which indicated that the police were investigating the incident.

He left the television on and went about sorting through the stack of documents in front of him.

Hernando had a smile on his face as he thought about the gold coins he would receive. He would have 80,000 US dollars. Less than he had originally calculated, but he could still keep his plan. He would have enough money to hire the airplane to take him to Mexico City. He would find another young lover and spend the rest of his life in leisure. Forty gold coins do not take up much space.

He looked up when he heard his door open. He watched as Rosalina walked across the room and stopped in front of his desk.

"While you were on the telephone, you received a call from a Mario Ricardo. He was calling from a city called Bogotá. He said that you would do well to return his call. He did not sound friendly."

When she had finished talking, she turned on her heels and marched back toward the still open door.

Hernando leaned back in his chair and reached for a cigar from the leather holder on his desk. He looked over to the window and studied the skyline as he lit it. Clouds of bluish-colored smoke began to form above him as he puffed continually for nearly a minute.

"What do these Colombians want to talk about? Why are they calling me now?" he asked himself.

He started to reach for the telephone on his desk and then changed his mind. He continued to puff on the huge Cuban cigar. The smoke was beginning to drift across the ceiling of the elegantly furnished office.

Again, he reached for the phone. This time he dialed the number written on the small piece of paper that Rosalina had given him.

A sweet voice on the other end of the line answered, "Executive Offices."

"This is Hernando Banderas in Guatemala City. I am returning Señor Mario Ricardo's call."

After a long silence, Hernando heard a voice.

"Banderas, this is Mario Ricardo. The people I represent are demanding that you cease shipping any of your products into the United States. You are interfering with my people's operations, and they will not tolerate it anymore. Do we understand each other?"

"Señor Ricardo, are you threatening me? Do you know who I am? Do your people know who I am?"

"We know much about you. Take my warning and retire. Do it now and stay alive."

Hernando heard the familiar click as Mario Ricardo hung up his phone.

30

Dan and Randy had been driving for nearly thirty minutes when Randy slowed down and pointed to a plain block building on the corner just ahead. The sign on the building read TGV Channel 3.

Before they had left Dan's hotel following breakfast, Randy had mentioned that Channel 3 was the city's primary source for local news.

When they walked into the TV station's lobby area, Randy motioned for Dan to take a seat. He walked up to the counter and asked to see the station manager, Pedro Jenaro. The receptionist walked over to the telephone and punched in an extension number.

Less than a minute later, a man of about sixty came out of his office located at the end of the hallway. He walked directly to Randy. He was a man of medium height and build, standing at about five-foot-ten.

"Hello, Señor Johnson. For what do I have the pleasure of your visit? I have not seen you for at least two years."

"Hello, Pedro. I want you to meet a friend of mine. This is Señor Branson from the United States. He would like to purchase some television time from your station."

"Excellent. Please follow me to my office. I am always happy to meet new people from your country."

Pedro led Dan and Randy into an office that looked like it could barely hold three people, with only a small metal desk, a desk chair, and one chair facing the desk. No other office equipment or fixtures were seen, not even pictures on the wall or anything on the small desk, except for a telephone.

"Excuse me while I bring in another chair."

Pedro placed another chair alongside Dan. He motioned for Randy to sit down and then slid into his chair behind the desk.

"I need to apologize for these cramped conditions. We are in the process of remodeling this entire building.

"My office is actually upstairs on the second floor. I assure you it is nearly ten times the size of this room. This room was actually a storeroom before I chose to use it as a temporary room for me to occupy.

"Mr. Branson, what can I do for you?"

"I'll be straightforward with you, Pedro. My daughter, Mattie, came to Guatemala to work with a missionary at a facility located at Santa Inés. Yesterday morning, she was kidnapped while she was doing her morning run. She was with two other girls that accompanied her to this country. Those two girls managed to get away. I arrived at your city just last night.

"My intention is to purchase two thirty-second spots every hour, for the rest of today plus all of tomorrow until midnight. I wish to be able to record a message that will inform your public, as well as the kidnappers, that I am willing to pay whatever ransom they demand. I am only interested in the safe return of my daughter."

"Señor Branson, you are talking about a very expensive program. I have the deepest feelings for your position. I, too, have a young daughter. I would be as anxious as you to arrange for her safe return.

"In reviewing our advertising rates, I feel I can make a small adjustment to make this possible for you, but the package will still be very expensive. The best that I can offer you would be to reduce our charges to 760 quetzals for each thirty-second spot. If I calculate correctly, your cost would be approximately 100 US dollars each time your message is broadcast. Are you in a position to pay that kind of cost?"

"Yes, I am able to do that. How soon can I get started?"

"Let me call in my program director. I will ask him to start on your request immediately. Do you have a picture of your daughter? That would be helpful."

"I have a picture of her, but I have made the decision not to broadcast her photo. I am confident that we will probably receive many counterfeit calls. The only way that I can be certain that I am talking to the real kidnappers will be to have them answer certain questions."

"Dan, I agree with you," Randy said "You and I need to sit down and go over the script and dialog for the pitch. If we spend an hour coming up with the right words, we can increase our chances of hearing from the real kidnappers. Pedro, can you give Dan and me a place where we can design and perfect his presentation?"

"Certainly, please follow me. I want you to meet my program director. I want him to be ready to post your spot on our station the minute you have it prepared."

Pedro led them down the hallway to the stairs leading to the upper floors.

"Please watch your steps, gentlemen. Remember that we are still under construction. The program director's office is on the second floor."

Pedro stopped in front of an office that was at least four times the size of the small room from which they had just come. He motioned for Dan and Randy to follow him through the doorway.

"Gentlemen, this is Ramon Severo, my program director. Ramon, this is Señor Dan Branson and Señor Randy Johnson. They are both Americans. They wish to have us broadcast spots every thirty minutes for the rest of today and all of tomorrow until midnight.

"They will be working on their presentation in the new conference room. When they are ready to have their material broadcast, I have told them that you will help them by producing their message and getting it onto our schedules."

Ramon nodded. He shook hands with Dan and Randy and then led them to the conference room. He told them to use the room and any of its facilities to prepare their material. Then he turned and left Dan and Randy alone in the room.

"Tell me, Randy, what do you suggest for the content of my spot? I'm really not good at this. I have never had to do anything like this before."

"I will put down on paper what I have in mind. Obviously, you will have the opportunity to change or alter what I write. I've seen lots of these pleas. Some work and some don't. I want to be sure that what I recommend includes the right statements."

Randy went through at least twenty sheets of paper before he handed a sheet to Dan.

"Dan, I think this is what you need to say. I will work with you on how to sift out the phonies as well as recognize the real bad guys."

Dan read the script out loud: "My name is Dan Branson. I am an American. My daughter was kidnapped yesterday morning. If you are the kidnappers, please be advised that I am in a position to pay any financial demands you make. You can contact me at the Barceló Hotel by calling the hotel and asking for me by name. I will have several questions that you must answer in order for me to determine if you have my daughter. I am not interested in referring this to the authorities. Everything will be handled with extreme discretion."

The two men studied the script for several minutes. Then, Dan decided that the script was good. He looked at Randy and gave him a thumbs-up sign.

"Randy, you've got it nailed. Now, we should work on the right questions to ask."

"We can work on that later. Let's get this on the screen. I don't want to waste any more time," Randy replied.

Dan and Randy walked down the hallway and entered the program director's office.

"I believe I am ready. I have my script prepared. What do you want me to do next?"

"Gentlemen, please follow me. I will take you to one of our recording rooms. I will have a cameraman come in and record what you wish to broadcast."

Dan and Randy followed Ramon into yet another room. It had insulation panels on all four sides.

"Señor Branson, please take a seat on the other side of that long table. I will go and get my cameraman."

As directed, Dan sat down on the opposite side of the table. The cameraman entered the room with a large video camera resting on his right shoulder. The man did not speak English. Ramon stood for a moment talking to the man in Spanish and then turned back to face Dan.

"Señor Branson, the light will be bright. Do not look at the camera. Read your script, which I have enlarged and placed on the wall above the cameraman. Can you see your script? Are you ready?"

Dan nodded his head, indicating that he was ready. The cameraman flipped a switch. Lights all around the room came on. Ramon pointed his finger at Dan.

Dan read the script with a firm tone of conviction in his voice. They did not need to record Dan's message the second time. He nailed it the first time.

31

Hernando Banderas was sitting at his desk when the television on the wall behind him caught his attention. He spun around in his chair and stared at the face of the man on the screen. This was the father of the girl that Felipe and Garcia had captured near the town of Santa Inés.

This American man on the screen was offering to pay any amount for the return of his daughter. This, he thought, had presented him with a way to, as the saying goes, work both ends toward the middle.

He would call this man and arrange for him to pay a ransom. He would demand $100,000 in gold coins for his daughter. Hernando had no intention of turning the girl back to her father. He would collect the ransom from the American, and then he would still sell the girl to the Arab Sheiks.

He would wait until afternoon, and then he would call. He knew he could convince the man that he had his daughter.

* * *

Dan sat in his room glued to his television even though he could not understand most of what was being said on the screen. He had left the set on channel three, knowing that each time his spot was aired, he might receive a call.

He saw the ad again; Ramon was right on schedule. Exactly thirty minutes since the last broadcast directed at the kidnappers, it ran again.

He stared at the screen and watched as his voice in English boomed through the speakers of his set. As he spoke on the screen, his message, in subtitles, was being displayed in Spanish, scrolling across the bottom of the screen.

He sat and watched as his spot disappeared, and the screen went back to the regular programming. He had become mesmerized by both the sound that he did not understand and the pictures that kept changing.

Suddenly, his phone rang. He jumped as though he had been shot and reached for the phone.

"This is Dan Branson."

"Señor, I am not very good at speaking English. I have the girl you say is your daughter. You will have to give me 10,000 American dollars, and I will bring her to you."

"Tell me, what is my daughter's name?"

After a long silence, Dan heard a click as the phone was hung up by the caller.

Dan sighed and leaned back against the headboard attached to the wall behind his bed. Then, the phone rang again.

"This is Dan Branson."

"Hi, Dan. It's Randy. Have you had any calls?"

"Yes, I just had one, but it was a phony. They hung up when I asked them to tell me Mattie's name."

"I'm afraid you may get a lot of that. Hang in there. Before too long, the bad guys will respond. You'll know you've got the right guy when he can answer your questions. I'll check with you a little later in the day. You have my cell number. Call me as soon as you make contact with the real kidnappers."

* * *

Mattie and Amy were talking in the dining room when Isabella hurried into the room with an excited look on her face.

"Follow me. You must see this."

The two girls followed Isabella into a small room that she referred to as her study where a television was on the wall that was transmitting the local news in Spanish.

"I have one of those units that will let me record and play back programs. Let me run this back so that you can see what I called you to watch. She held a remote control in her hand. The girls watched as she ran the program back. Suddenly, Mattie let out a yell.

"*STOP! That's my dad!*" The three women watched and listened as Dan presented his plea to the kidnappers. Mattie jumped up and asked to use the phone.

"My dear, we can't call. Señor Banderas has our telephone lines tapped. Cell phones will not work this far out of the city. I know they listen every time I make a call. I also know that one of my gardeners is one of his people. He is very quiet and never talks to me. I see him talking on one of the extensions whenever I am in the gardens."

"If you call your father, they will move you immediately. Trust me, they are listening."

"I'm glad your father is here. Perhaps his message will reach Señor Banderas, and maybe he will heed to your father's offer."

* * *

Dan received, all told, nine calls in a period of five hours. His spot had been broadcasting since nine in the morning. In every case, the caller would hang up as soon as Dan would ask a question that only the kidnappers could answer. He was getting ready to walk out the door to have lunch when the phone rang again.

"This is Dan Branson. Who is calling?"

"I will not give you my name. I have your daughter. I am calling from a cell phone that you cannot trace. Are you willing to pay me 100,000 dollars in gold coins for the return of your daughter?"

"Yes, I will pay. First, you must answer a question for me. What is the name of my daughter's horse?"

"I do not know this. I will call you back very soon with the answer to your question."

Dan heard the caller hang up. He sat down on the edge of his bed and stared at the phone.

* * *

The three women were back in the kitchen drinking coffee when they heard the phone ring again. Isabella smiled at Mattie, rose, and walked to the phone.

"Señora Coronado, this is Señor Banderas. I am considering sending the new girl back to her father. You must ask her the name of her horse. If she will tell me that, I will send her to her father."

"I understand, Hernando. I have been watching the television too. I will ask the girl the question you want."

Isabella laid the phone down and approached Mattie.

"I need to know the name of your horse."

"My horse's name is Snickers."

Isabella nodded, walked back to the phone, and picked it up.

"Hernando, what assurance will you give me that you will release the girl if I tell you the name of her horse?"

"I do not need to tell you anything. I believe that you know that I can have you disposed of and no one will ever know what happened. Tell me the name of her horse."

"She says that the name of her horse is Snickers."

Hernando Banderas did not say another word. Isabella heard him hang up the phone.

"What did he say? When will he release me? Suddenly you look very pale. Tell me, what did he say to you?"

"He said that he could have me killed, and no one would ever know about it."

* * *

Hernando Banderas dialed Dan's hotel and, again, asked for his room.

"This is Dan Branson."

"Your daughter's horse is named Snickers. Now, I will tell you how you can get your daughter back. Listen carefully as I will not repeat myself. Your daughter is safe. She has not been harmed. She will be returned to you when you can tell me that you have the gold coins that I am demanding. Do you understand?"

"Yes, I understand. How will I let you know that I have the coins?"

"You will have the television station quit broadcasting your message immediately. You will obtain 50 Austrian Philharmonic one-ounce gold coins. When you have the coins in your possession, you will tell the people at the television station to announce every thirty minutes that 'Mr. Golden has arrived in Guatemala City.' Do you understand my instructions?"

"Yes, I understand. I will do as you say."

Dan heard the line disconnect. He reached down and pushed the stop button on the small tape recorder that Randy had provided that had recorded every message that he had received on his hotel room phone. He picked up the phone receiver again and dialed the cell phone number Randy had provided.

"Hello Dan, I recognized the number. What have you got?"

"He called. He has my daughter. He wants 50 Austrian gold coins."

"Have you got the gold coins he is asking for?"

"No, but I think I know where I can get them."

"I'll be over in a few minutes. We'll have some lunch and talk about how you're going to make this happen."

32

Dan and Randy had lunch in the hotel restaurant. They agreed that Dan must work fast to obtain the gold that was being demanded. Randy discouraged Dan from bringing the authorities into the picture as he had very little confidence in them. He was not certain as to who was loyal to the administration and who was connected with the underworld. Dan would pay the ransom and get Mattie back.

When he had finished lunch with Randy, Dan went back to his room, dug out his satellite phone, and dialed his home number. Jessie quickly answered the phone.

"Jessie, we have made contact with the people who have Mattie. They are demanding a ransom of 50 gold coins. Not just any gold coins; they want Austrian Philharmonics. Jessie, are you following me? Please write that down."

"Yes, tell me what to do."

"I hope you are not too attached to that Remington bronze thing we have sitting on our coffee table. I have thought that perhaps we could sell it to that guy in Great Falls. Remember the guy who called us when he found out that we had it? That would get us the gold coins we need to ransom Mattie."

"I remember. How do I get ahold of him?"

"Where are you right now?"

"I'm in the kitchen. Where do you want me?"

"Go into my office, and pick up the phone."

In less than a minute, Jessie walked down the hallway and entered Dan's office. She picked up his desk phone and then clicked the off button on the one she was carrying from the kitchen.

"I'm here. Tell me what to do."

"Look in the top right-hand drawer. See if you can locate a little black book. I think it says 'day planner' on the front."

"I got it. What am I looking for?"

"Thumb through the pages. I wrote the guy's name on one of the pages when he called. I can't remember his name, but I believe I wrote down 'Remington' beside his name."

"I got it, Dan. Do you want me to read you the number?"

"No. I want you to see if you can locate this guy. Tell him what has happened and see if he is still interested. I have no idea what the thing is worth. Tell him we need to get at least $100,000."

"I'm going to see if I can find a gold dealer here in Guatemala City. If I can find one, then I can purchase the coins here. If not, I will have to have you call around until you find someone with those particular coins."

"We are already one in the afternoon here. You are a couple of hours earlier. I will call you back at five o'clock this afternoon my time. That will make it three, your time."

"OK, Dan, I got it. Sweetheart, I love you. Please get Mattie back for me."

"I love you, too. I'm working on it. We'll make this happen. I know the Lord understands where we're at with these guys. Wait for my call."

Dan turned off his satellite phone and placed it back into his B-4 bag. He went back to the nightstand next to his bed and pulled out the local telephone directory. He opened the directory, only to find that everything was in Spanish. He put the directory back in the drawer, picked up the phone, and dialed a familiar number.

"Hi, Dan. How are we doing?"

"Randy, I need to see if I can find a gold dealer here in Guatemala City. I need to buy fifty Austrian Philharmonic one-ounce gold coins."

"Wow. Lots of luck. I'll be over in about thirty minutes. You're going to need some help on the phone. I speak the language, so maybe I can be of some help."

"Thanks, Randy. I think you know I can't make all of this happen without your help. I'll see you when you get here."

Randy spent the better part of three hours on the telephone. He had called every gold and coin dealer in Guatemala as well as Belize and Mexico City. In every case, the coins would be available, but not for at least three days. In all cases, the dealers would have to send for the coins. Dan and Randy had exhausted every possibility on their end.

At five o'clock, Dan took out his satellite phone and dialed home. Jessie immediately answered.

"Hi, Jessie. Did you locate our guy on the bronze?"

"Yes, and he said he wants to buy it. He said he thought it is maybe worth much more than the $100,000, but that would be all he could afford to pay. He said that he would go to his bank in the morning and borrow the money. Funds will be available to wire at ten in the morning, Montana time."

"Perfect. I am having trouble finding anyone that has fifty of those Austrian gold coins. Have you made any calls? Were you able to locate anyone with those particular coins?"

"Actually, I did. A company in Los Angeles has them. The company is called Goldex They said that they could possibly ship them out tomorrow, and you would have them on Thursday. Will that work?"

"Yes. I think that will work. Everything has to fit together perfectly. I am a little worried about the timing on all of this. Maybe you had better call our banker in Bend and tell him what's happening since you are only about three there. If he can get hold of this Goldex outfit and guarantee payment, perhaps they can get the coins shipped to me so that I will have them on Thursday. ₴ Can you do that?"

"Consider it done. Give me a call back in an hour, and I'll give you an update. Dan, are they going to give us back Mattie if we give them the gold?"

"Sweetheart, you and I both know that we are dealing with very bad people. However, I have every reason to believe that we will have her back as soon as they have their ransom."

33

Hernando Banderas sat at his desk and listened to the program on channel three. He would hope to get his gold from this Dan Branson on Thursday. That way, he could be ready to ship the two girls off to Africa on Friday.

This American fool will lose his daughter and the 100,000 US dollars he will have to pay for the gold coins, Banderas thought. Everything was working out for him. Soon, he would be sitting in a new home in Mexico City. He would never have to work again. He would marry a beautiful young Mexican girl and be very happy for the rest of his life.

He lit another cigar and walked over to the large window overlooking the city. Again, he was puffing so much that the room was filling with pungent cigar smoke. He stood in front of the picture window for a while before he heard what he was waiting for.

"I have a special message for Mr. Golden who is scheduled to arrive in Guatemala City on Thursday. If you are friend of Mr. Golden, please call."

Hernando walked back over to his desk and slid into his chair. He picked up the telephone and dialed the number of the Barceló Hotel and asked for Dan's room.

"This is Dan Branson."

"You will listen carefully. I will call you Thursday evening at seven o'clock. I will tell you where to place the gold coins. You must follow my directions if you want to see your daughter again. Do you understand?"

"Yes, I understand. You must also understand that I will not receive the 50 Austrian gold coins until Thursday afternoon. They are being delivered to me here at the hotel. I will take them to whatever place you will direct me to on Thursday evening."

* * *

"Hey Mattie, your old man must have a lot of bucks. He is offering to pay any ransom that is demanded. You're really a lucky gal; he must love you a lot. Do you suppose you could get him to adopt me?"

"Amy, I don't have any idea how Dad is going to come up with the ransom. He is not my real dad. My real dad was killed in Iraq before I was born. He married my mom and adopted me. He is the only dad I have ever known, and we have become a very close family. God has really blessed us.

"You mentioned adoption. Amy, you could become a child of God. All you have to do is ask Him. Once you give your life to the Lord, He not only makes you His child, He forgives all of your sins. You'll become a totally new person. He writes your name in His book, and you'll be with Him in Heaven."

"That sounds nice coming from you. I don't really think that He would be interested in somebody who has made as much of a mess of her life as I have. The only time I remember anything about God is when my grandmother used to take me to church every Easter."

"I just wish I had a dad like yours. My dad doesn't care what happens to me. You are going to go home, and I am going to be taken to Africa to become some Sheik's playmate."

"Amy, you don't know that. God can do so much for you when you give Him your life. I accepted Jesus, God's son, when I was a little girl. I know that His angels are watching over me right now."

Isabella sat quietly listening to the interaction between the two girls as tears began to make their way down her cheeks.

"I must tell both of you that I haven't always looked to the Lord to guide me in my life. When He took my little girl away from me, I became very bitter. I didn't pay any more attention to God and His teachings."

"Then when my husband died in a plane crash, I became even more bitter. Finally, after a year, I recognized that He never left me, nor did He forsake me. I can tell you of many times in my life when I just know that He came to my rescue."

"I was just like Mattie. When I was just nine years old, I accepted Jesus and became a Christian. I know my husband was a Christian, and I also remember when my daughter, Sophia, knelt in our garden and asked Jesus into her heart. I agree with Mattie God knows what's happening right here in this big old house."

* * *

Dan heard the knock on his hotel room door. When he swung the door open, he saw Randy standing with a solemn look on his face.

"I've been talking with Ed Harris and some of the guys at Langley. They're telling me that you have to be real careful about how you make the exchange. They say these guys usually try to grab their money and then not give you back your daughter.

"I don't know what you have said to these people. I would like it if you and I were to discuss some options. I don't mean to not give them the ransom. I mean we have to be sure we get your daughter."

"You're right, Randy. I have thought of the possibility that they may try to pull something. I just don't know if I am in a position to have many options."

"How can you take so much time to be my support person? I can't believe that you don't have somebody breathing down your neck, telling you to get back to work. By the way, what do you do for your cover job?"

"Actually, as far as the people down here are concerned, I am a consultant and a liaison for the U.S. Department of Agriculture. I think I told you about Blake Donavan and Grant Adams. They are the two guys also with the company that work with me."

"Agriculture consultant? I figured you and your two buddies came from some spy school located deep in the woods of Virginia. What do you guys know about farming?"

"I grew up on a sugar beet and feed corn farm in central Minnesota. My partners both grew up on wheat farms in the Dakotas. Don't sell us short. It's actually a pretty good cover. We get to watch most of the import-export activity that takes place throughout all of Central America.

"Let's talk about how we're going to be sure to get your daughter back. What kind of arrangements have you made so far?"

"Randy, so far we haven't got anything solid to go on. This guy told me that he will call me and tell me where to bring the money. That's all I know."

34

The Thursday morning sun was shining in the window of Dan's hotel room. He looked out the window and surveyed the city. A heavy layer of smog was covering the entire city. The telephone on the nightstand next to his bed rang only once before he grabbed it.

"Hello, this is Dan Branson."

"Señor Branson, this is the front desk. A gentleman here says he has a delivery for you. He will need your signature. Do you want me to send him up or would you rather come down here?"

"Tell the man to wait right there. I will be down in just a minute."

Dan looked around his room to be sure that he had not left anything lying around that would attract attention. By now, everyone in the hotel knew about the gentleman staying in the hotel whose daughter had been kidnapped.

The young man standing next to the desk was wearing a brown uniform with a logo over the shirt pocket that said he was with a well-known courier service. As Dan walked up to the desk, the clerk pointed him out to the courier.

"Señor Branson, I must have you sign here for this package."

The young man pushed a clipboard that was lying on the counter toward Dan. He was clutching a small box in his other hand. Dan signed the form attached to the clipboard, and the courier handed him the package, turned, and headed for the door.

THE VILLA

Dan looked around the room and observed that only two other people were in the lobby. One was an elderly woman who was standing by the window studying the people passing by. The other was a bellman who appeared to be busy sorting through a box of keys.

Dan took the small box that was about the size of a book and went straight to his room. He broke the seal on the box and examined its contents. In it were five plastic tubes that were about one inch high and nearly an inch and a half in diameter.

Dan opened the tubes one at a time and poured out their contents. In front of him were 50 brilliant gold coins. He examined the coins and noted a picture of numerous musical instruments on one side. The coin read, "Repulik Osterreich – 2000 Schilling." The count was exactly 50 coins. The current market value for these 50 coins was 100,000 US dollars.

* * *

Hernando Banderas parked his car in the underground garage beneath the Hernandez Building and took the elevator to the top floor. He used his key to open the door to his private office. He looked at his watch and noted the time was eight at night and that it had been dark for nearly an hour. He took exactly one hour to drive from the little town of Treparzo to his office.

He sat down at his desk, reached into his pocket, and pulled out his cell phone. He dialed the number of the Barceló 4 and asked for Dan Branson. He had decided to make the call short, assuming that the authorities may be trying to trace his call.

"Mr. Branson, listen carefully. I will not repeat myself. At midnight tonight—not one minute before—you are to bring my gold to an abandoned church located near the small town of Treparzo. You must come alone. If I see anyone else, you will never see your daughter again. I will be watching.

"When you see the sign, Treparzo, look to the right, and you will see the ruins of an ancient church that is several centuries old. You cannot miss it—it has a steeple with a cross on top that is still very visible. You should allow one hour to drive there from your hotel.

"Go into the church and then down the rock stairway that leads to the underground. Take a battery torch. I believe you call it a flashlight. Place my gold on the wooden table between the two candles that I have burning on the table. When I have retrieved my gold, I will leave the directions on the table for you to find your daughter. You may come back to the church at two in the morning for those directions, and not one minute earlier."

Hernando closed the lid to his cell phone and looked at his watch. The call had taken less than a minute. He knew that would not be long enough for anyone to trace his call.

Dan hung up the phone in his room and pushed the small button to stop his recorder. He looked at his watch; it was just a little past eight. He had four hours to get the gold to the church in Treparzo.

He had spent most of the afternoon with Randy. They had discussed all of the various possibilities and options. Finally, Dan made the decision that he would have to take his chances and go it alone. The decision was over Randy's objections. Dan had repeated several times during their conversations that the Lord knew what was happening. Dan knew that he would have to put his trust in Him in order to get Mattie back.

Randy had offered to let Dan drive his Suburban, and he would crouch down in the back. He was confident that if they captured the kidnapper they could get him to tell them where Mattie was being held. Dan declined. Again he told Randy that everything was in the Lord's hands.

Dan agreed to let Randy loan him his car. He wouldn't have time to rent a car. Randy was determined to wait at the hotel until he heard from Dan, who would take his satellite phone and call Randy the minute he found out where Mattie was being held.

* * *

The sky had become overcast and it was pitch black out when Dan climbed into Randy's Suburban, heading for the little town of Treparzo. He had studied the map with Randy and laid out a route. With the map and Randy's GPS, he was confident that he would find the little village without trouble. He left the hotel at a quarter to eleven and felt sure he had allowed himself sufficient time to get to the church.

Just before midnight, Dan stopped the Suburban directly in front of the old church. The man who had called him was correct; it truly was the ruins of a church that had to be at least 200 years old. Most of the building had fallen to the ground.

The entrance became visible when the lights of Randy's Suburban illuminated the ancient structure. Dan studied the building for a minute before he turned off the headlights, picked up the box containing the gold, grabbed his flashlight, and started for the entrance.

Dan stumbled twice, trying to find a staircase to what the man had referred to as the underground. Finally, he stepped around a pile of stone and located the opening that appeared to lead down into darkness. He stepped carefully down the rock steps. He saw a glow ahead of him. When he reached the bottom step, he saw a wooden table that was pushed against the rock wall; two glowing candles were on the table.

Dan walked to the table, opened the box, and poured out the gold coins that he had removed from their plastic containers. He stepped back to look at the gold brilliantly displayed in the middle of the table, turned, and walked back up the rock stairs.

Dan looked at his watch and saw that the time was ten minutes past twelve. He had made the decision earlier that he would follow the kidnapper's instructions. He drove the Suburban into the little village and parked near the town square where he saw no signs of anyone or any activity since it was the middle of the night.

Hernando had watched from a distance as Dan pulled up in front of the old church ruins. He had parked his Mercedes out of sight behind an abandoned building. He watched Dan as he went into the ancient building and then watched him again as he left ten minutes later.

He sat in his car for nearly thirty minutes. Then he left his car parked where it was and walked the 200 meters to the church entrance.

Hernando had a flashlight that he used to guide his steps through the rubble filling the inside of the church. He went directly to the familiar entrance to the underground. When he reached the bottom step, he let out a gasp as he saw the sparkling pile of gold coins. He walked to the table and stared down at the coins in amazement.

"Hello, Hernando. I have been waiting for you."

Hernando spun around and found himself staring at a dark-haired man who looked to be in his late forties. He was wearing a black-hooded priest's robe. He was tall, well over six feet, and was of medium build. His eyes caught Hernando's attention. They seemed to be ablaze, deep, penetrating, almost frightening.

"Who are you? What are you doing here? Are you a priest?"

"I am here to talk to you about what you are doing. I have been watching you. Does your wife know where you are and what you are doing?"

"What do you know about me or my wife? I am here to collect my gold. Step aside and let me be on my way."

"Do you know that God is going to punish you for all of the evil that you have done? The drugs that you sell on the streets around the world have destroyed many lives.

"This evil deed that you are doing now—kidnapping those girls—will lead to more damnation for you. If you do not turn to God, He will surely be the one that will see you burning in hell."

Hernando was trembling now. The sweat was beginning to run down his cheeks.

"I don't know who you are. I will take my gold and leave."

"Let's just say I am a messenger from God. If you try to take that gold on the table, you may see the wrath of God poured out on you before you can get to that Mercedes of yours that is parked behind the abandoned building across the road."

Hernando's eyes were wide as he stared at this messenger of God known as Michael, the Archangel. He was no longer trembling; he was shaking. The sweat that was formerly trickling down his face had now totally drenched his shirt. He began to back away from the table with the glittering gold, still lying where Dan had placed it.

Hernando stared into Michael's penetrating eyes. Suddenly, he turned and half-stumbled, half-ran up the stairs. Michael could hear him stumbling across the debris as he ran out of the entrance, across the road, and to his Mercedes. He started his car, jammed it into gear, and raced back toward the city.

* * *

Dan stared out of the window of Randy's Suburban and looked up into the sky. The overcast had gone away, and now millions of stars could be seen. He had sat for nearly two hours. He had prayed several times, making the same plea each time he prayed. His last prayer, less than a minute ago, was asking God to be with Jessie and Danny as they sat waiting for him to call.

He looked at his watch and noted that it was quarter to two in the morning. Following the instructions of the kidnappers, he had waited until two before returning to the old church to find the directions that would lead him to where Mattie was being held.

Now was the time. He started the engine and drove quickly back to the ancient ruins. He grabbed his flashlight and ran through the entrance. He stepped carefully around the debris and then went down the steps to the underground. He caught his breath and went weak when he first saw all of the gold, still glistening in the light from the candles.

"Hi, cowboy. I've been waiting for you."

"Michael, is that you?"

"Yes, it's me; who did you think would be sent to get you out of trouble ... *again*? I couldn't leave this up to just any angel, now could I?"

"Praise the Lord!"

"Well, cowboy, you've got that right. Let's take our gold and go get Mattie."

"Do you know where she is? The guy told you where they are keeping our girl?"

"Oh, yeah, I already knew where she was. He didn't have time to do much talking when the time came for him to leave. I'm going to drive. You would never find your way to the plantation, which is about an hour from here. Do you think you should give Jessie a call?"

"I think I'll wait until we have Mattie. I imagine she is asleep since the time is midnight at home. Where did you get that outfit you are wearing? And what made him leave the gold behind?"

"I found this outfit in that wooden closet in the corner of that room where you put the gold. Don't you think it looks pretty good on me?"

"What made the guy leave without the gold?"

Michael looked over at Dan, winked, and then said, "I think maybe it was something that I said to him."

They had been driving down the road for several minutes at a pretty fast rate of speed, when Dan looked over at Michael. He let out a big sigh when he noticed that Michael was leaning back in his seat with his eyes closed. His hands were in his lap, not on the steering wheel.

35

"Wake up, cowboy. We're here."

Dan opened his eyes and looked ahead as they drove under the stone arch entrance that read, "Villa de las Flores." Michael, now wide awake, steered the Suburban up to the front of the mansion and stopped.

Dan got out on the passenger's side and sprinted up the steps. Before he could reach for the heavy rope that served as a door bell, the door swung open.

"You must be Mattie's father. I am Isabella Coronado. I've been looking after your daughter. Give me a minute, and I will fetch her for you."

Before she could turn to walk to the ancient elevator, Dan saw Mattie coming down the stairs, taking two or three steps at a time. She screamed and literally jumped into Dan's outstretched arms. Tears were flowing down the cheeks of all three of them.

"We need to call your mom. I'll dial the number, and you can let her know you're OK."

Dan took the satellite phone from the pocket of his jacket and dialed their home. Jessie, sound asleep, instantly became alert. When she heard Mattie's voice, she screamed loudly, then sobbed. She then relaxed to listen to her daughter's voice.

"Hi, Mom. It's me. Dad just showed up, and I am fine. Everything is going to be fine now. I love you so much! I wish I were there to hug you. Hang on. I'll give you back to Dad."

Dan and Jessie talked for several minutes before he promised to call her in the morning. Dan closed the cover on his satellite phone and turned to face Isabella.

"I don't believe that you've played a part of this horrible affair. So, how did you manage to get my girl?"

"That's a long story, Señor Branson. Perhaps we should go into the kitchen. I will make some coffee. Do you need to make more phone calls?"

"Yes, I need to call my friend, Randy Johnson. He is at my hotel waiting for me to call."

Isabella nodded that she understood as Dan, once again, took out his satellite phone and dialed his hotel. When he was connected with his room, Randy answered.

Dan gave him a brief rundown on what had taken place. He told him to take a nap in his room. He told Randy that he would bring his car back to the hotel after daylight.

When Dan had finished his call, he looked to see another young girl standing beside Mattie. He looked at Isabella and then at Mattie. Amy wore a big smile on her face.

"Hi. You must be Mattie's dad. I am Mattie's friend. I want you to adopt me. I need a new dad."

Both Mattie and Isabella were chuckling at Amy's statement. They started for the kitchen as Isabella stopped and turned to Dan.

"Shouldn't we ask your driver to come in and join us for coffee?"

Before Dan could answer, Isabella turned and walked back to the large front door and looked out to Randy's Suburban, but no one was in the car.

"I saw you get out of the car on the passenger's side. What has become of your driver?"

"I guess he didn't want to stick around."

"Who drove you here, Dad?"

"Somebody you haven't met, but you've heard a lot about. Our friend, Michael, the Archangel, helped me find you and get you back. Michael also drove me here. Although he was the driver, he slept most of the way. I honestly didn't know how to get here."

"Wow, Michael came through again! That is so fantastic. I wish I could have met him. I know that someday I will." The four of them sat around the table in the middle of the kitchen and chatted for nearly an hour. Finally, Amy rose up from where she was sitting and stretched.

"I need to go back to bed and get a few more Zzz's. I suspect now that your dad has sprung you out of the trap that the bad guys, whoever they are, will be back. I figure they're going to be pretty desperate. They want to grab me and send me off to those Arab sheiks."

"I don't think you have to worry about that, Amy. I'm pretty confident that the 'bad guys, as you call them, are no longer a threat. I think we can thank our friend Michael for that," Dan said.

"You mean I won't be taken to become some Sheik's girlfriend? Am I really not going to be sold?"

"That's right. You are no longer in danger."

"Mr. Branson, will you be here when I wake up? I really need help. I need someone to help me figure out what to do with the rest of my life."

"Señor Branson, you look to me like you haven't slept well for several days," Isabella said. "I have six bedrooms that are not being used. Won't you lay down for a short time and get some rest? A shower is right next to your room. I believe we will all make more sense if we have a few hours of rest."

"That's probably a good idea, Señora Coronado. I don't believe I should try to drive back into the city during the middle of the night. We're just now approaching four in the morning. If we all get three or four more hours of shut-eye, we would all feel better. I think my friend in my hotel room will take a long snooze on my bed. He can't go anywhere. I have his Suburban."

Isabella led Dan to one of the rooms on the second floor. She apologized to Dan, saying that it was one of her smaller rooms. Actually, it was at least three times larger than his hotel room. She pointed to the door in the back corner of the room, telling Dan that it was a complete bathroom with a large stall shower.

* * *

Dan slept soundly for nearly four hours. He woke when he heard a pounding on his door.

"Rise and shine, Dad. The coffee is on. We're all waiting for you in the kitchen. You've got time for a quick shower. Breakfast will be on the table in twenty minutes. Don't be late."

He really did feel refreshed. His sleep for the past four nights had been very troubled. He had tossed and turned constantly. When dawn had come, he couldn't remember if he had slept at all.

Dan quickly showered. He went down the long winding staircase to the main floor and then followed the wonderful aromas coming from the kitchen.

All three women were waiting for him with big smiles on their faces. Mattie got up from her chair, went to her father, and hugged him.

"I love you so much, Dad." She turned to Isabella and Amy and said, "Ladies, I am going to ask my dad to say a blessing over this food. I know he will be thanking the Lord for delivering all of us out of the perils that we have been living under."

Dan's prayer was not brief, nor was it long. He prayed like he was alone, kneeling before God's altar. The ladies could tell that this man had put his life and his heart on the line for his daughter. He truly was a man of God.

Amy sat quietly as Mattie and her father related their life and experiences at Triple Peaks Ranch. She was mesmerized with the love that seemed to radiate between them. She had never seen nor experienced that kind of love in her family.

Isabella also sat quietly while the father and his daughter interacted and reunited. Amy, also watching Dan and Mattie, looked at Mattie's father with an inquisitive expression on her face.

"Mr. Branson, Mattie has told us that you went to South America a few years ago to assist a rancher who was being harassed by a cartel. What prompted you to travel several thousand miles to help someone you didn't even know?"

"Amy, many years ago when I was a small boy, I gave my life to God. I asked His Son, Jesus Christ, to take over my life. I committed myself to serving Him whenever He called

"God's angel told those people down there that I would help them. They called me and told me what the angel said. I knew God wanted me to help them, so I went to South America."

"What's with all this angel talk? Are you all trying to tell me that angels actually talk to people?" Amy asked as she looked at the other three at the table.

Isabella began to nod her head up and down and was moving her shoulders forward and back. Then she placed both hands on the table, looked at each person on the table, and leaned forward in her chair. She had a look of determination on her face.

"I must tell all of you what happened in my life. I have never told anyone about this. You are the first people in this world I have ever shared this with."

She sat upright in her chair. Her shoulders were squared as she began to speak.

"My little girl, Sophia, was only three when she died. My husband was only forty-two when he died. Both of them had given their hearts and their lives to the Lord. For a long time, I was very angry at God for taking my family away."

"When I was only nine years old, I gave my life to Jesus. One day when I was working in my garden, a man dressed as a peasant came to talk to me. I did not see him approach. I thought that a man showing up like that was very strange.

"This man said he was a messenger. He told me that God had a plan for my life. He said that my husband and my daughter were both with the Lord. We talked for quite a time. Then he prayed with me. Just before he left, he said his name was Angelo.

"Right after that man left, I rededicated my life to the Lord. Ever since that day, I have been waiting for our Lord to show me what he would have me do to serve Him."

As she finished speaking, Mattie reached for her father's hand and squeezed it. She looked into his eyes and smiled.

"What do you think, Dad? Our guy Angelo really has gotten around, hasn't he?"

"Wow, you guys," Amy said. "You're all beginning to give me goose bumps. Are you trying to tell me all of you know this same guy, Angelo? Mattie, is this the same Angelo you were telling me about the other day?"

"Amy, I am confident that we are talking about the very same man. My father will tell you that our family knows him *very* well. We refer to him as our family's guardian angel."

Dan was nodding his head. He knew exactly who Mattie was talking about. He recalled Angelo telling him to remember one particular Bible verse.

"Be not forgetful to entertain strangers:
for thereby some have entertained angels unawares."
(Hebrews 13:2)

"Dad, I talked to Charlene this morning. I told her I would be coming back to finish my tour with Alicia and Bethany. I hope you're not disappointed that I don't want to go straight home from here. Is that OK with you, Dad?"

Dan nodded that he understood what Mattie had just said. He knew that Jessie would understand, too.

"Amy, how about you and I take a walk on this beautiful morning? You and I have just had a ton of weight lifted from our shoulders," Mattie said as she rose from her chair.

Isabella rose from her seat and suggested that she show Dan the rest of her mansion. When they had toured the lower floors, Isabella ushered him into her vintage elevator and took him up to the third floor. They entered Mattie's room. Then Isabella led him into the bathroom to show him the magnificent spa-type bathroom.

"I think perhaps my Mattie probably really liked staying here. Isabella, this magnificent mansion and all the amenities are nothing short of spectacular."

"Señor Branson, it needs many repairs. I have been talking to Mattie about her friend Charlene. Her mission building is very old and also in terrible condition.

"I was thinking that this Charlene lady could move her orphanage and refuge here. What a wonderful place for the children and the women who are trying to reestablish their lives."

"Señora Coronado, I believe you're probably right. I haven't seen Charlene's mission, but I am sure it has nowhere near the potential and possibilities that your fantastic plantation could provide.

"If you're willing to commit yourself to doing what you have just suggested, you might find that the Lord would provide the resources."

"Señor Branson, I would estimate that I would need to 100,000 US dollars to accomplish that. I don't know how I could ever come up with that amount of money. It would be impossible."

Dan and Isabella walked over to the window. They both peered out onto the plantation's breathtaking gardens. Isabella placed one hand over her mouth and gasped as she pointed, with her other hand, to the far corner of the gardens. Mattie and Amy were kneeling in front of a fountain with a winged angel mounted on top. Amy had her hands folded and was bowing her head. Mattie, also bowing her head, had her hand on Amy's shoulder.

"Isabella, I think that Amy may choose to stay here and work with you. I think she is dedicating her life to Jesus Christ right now. I believe she will want to help you turn this place into the kind of facility you have just described.

"You know, you might want to consider that Amy just might possibly be God's plan to provide you with another daughter.

"I would like to have you walk with me to that Suburban we left out in front of your home early this morning. I have a little box that I believe the Lord would have me leave with you."

Isabella followed Dan to the Suburban. He opened the passenger door and picked up the small box that contained 50 gold coins. He knew their value to be exactly what Isabella had estimated she would need to bring her mansion up to the standards required to move Charlene's mission to Villa de las Flores. He handed the box to Isabella.

"Isabella, the gold in this little box is valued at 100,000 US dollars. This is God's money, not mine. I believe he wants you to have it. I also believe that Villa de las Flores is destined to be a very happy place."

36

When Dan and Mattie walked through the door of Charlene's mission, they were greeted by screams, waving arms, and giant hugs from Alicia and Bethany. Charlene stood a few feet away from the group, sobbing and shaking. She had managed to hold her feelings deep inside during the entire event. Now, the return of Mattie and the presence of Dan released her pent up emotions.

Eventually, everyone calmed down and listened intently as Mattie related her experiences since she was snatched away and taken to Isabella's villa. The three women were mesmerized with Mattie's experience.

When the excitement and emotions had subsided, Dan told the women that he had to return the Suburban and would come back to the mission as soon as he had explained all the events of the prior evening to Randy, who was still waiting at the Barceló Hotel.

* * *

"I have to tell you, cowboy, I don't doubt a word that you have said," Randy told Dan. "I have goose bumps just trying to fathom all that has happened. This guy, Michael, always seems to be around when you need him the most. I'm going to try and describe all of what has happened to my wife."

"Randy, you will never know just how much I appreciate all that you and your guys back at Langley have done for me. I know I would not have made it without you. Give my thanks to everyone involved. I'll give Ed a call as soon as I get back to the ranch."

The two men stood for a moment staring at each other, and then Dan reached forward and gave Randy a warm bear hug. Randy returned the hug, then stuck out his hand and shook Dan's hand firmly. He turned, waved, and headed for his Suburban.

An hour later, Dan guided his rental car along the road that led to Charlene Pearson's mission in Santa Inés. He had rented a car from a local car rental agency located just a block from his hotel.

Dan's mind wandered as he drove. He relived the experiences that had taken place since he received the news of Mattie's abduction. Again, the Lord had come to his rescue. He shook his head in amazement as he imagined seeing Michael standing in that dimly lit room beneath the old church. He had no doubt in his mind that the Lord was constantly looking after him and his family.

The three girls heard his car drive up and stop at the entrance to the mission. They ran out to greet him and looked in amazement at the large French SUV he was driving.

"Dad, where did you find that thing?"

"Hey, I got it because it has a GPS, and I wasn't sure that I could get back to Charlene's mission without the help of modern-day electronics."

"I think it's fantastic," Alicia said. "Can we take a ride in it?"

"That's my plan. I want to take all of you out to Isabella's plantation."

"Dad, do you plan to tell Charlene what Isabella said about turning her plantation into a new location for the mission?"

"No, I think I will leave that up to Isabella. She mentioned that she was thinking of making that decision, but I don't believe we should make an issue of what she said until she makes the announcement."

"Wow, if she does turn the Villa de las Flores into a mission, it would be spectacular. Just think of the impact that would have on her work," Bethany said.

"Well," Dan said, "let's see if Charlene wants to take a ride out to the plantation. She's heard Mattie describe the place. Now let's see what she thinks. Maybe everything will happen the way we want."

Charlene talked for a few minutes with Pablo about looking after the mission while she was gone. She looked at Dan and then indicated that she was ready to take the trip to visit the plantation where Mattie and Amy had been held captive.

* * *

Dan directed his rental car under the giant arch that read, Villa de las Flores. They wove their way down the long winding drive. All of the women, including Mattie, let out a gasp as the striking beauty of the magnificent villa came into view.

"This is a great place to be incarcerated," Alicia said with a giggle. "Can we get a look inside?"

"You people are going to love this place. Wait until you see all of the fantastic murals that are on the ceiling in every room," Mattie said. "This fantastic villa has been in the Coronado family for *three* generations. Before their daughter died, they grew pineapples and mangos in the field behind all of those trees. This place is huge."

Hearing their arrival, Isabella waited on the wide veranda at the top of the stairs. "Welcome to Villa de las Flores. I am sure Mattie has told you all about her stay here with me and Amy. Speaking of Amy, please come in. I want you to meet her. She is telling me she never wants to leave this place. She is very anxious to meet all of you."

Amy was standing in the entrance and walked over to Mattie, giving her a hug. "Welcome back, sister! I have missed our rap sessions. These must be the friends you have been telling me about."

Amy gave each of the ladies a hug and motioned for them to come inside. As they moved through the grand entrance and the spacious foyer, Charlene, Alicia, and Bethany had trouble keeping their mouths closed as they stared in awe at the scene developing in front of their eyes. They toured room after room, studying the magnificent art, furniture, and décor of each room. Finally, when they exited the elevator on the third floor and were directed into the room that Mattie had occupied, all three stopped short and surveyed the giant bedroom.

"Staying here was not easy, but I managed to tough it out for the past four days. Let me show you the bathroom I was *forced* to share with Amy," Mattie said, a grin on her face.

Mattie pushed open the wide, blue door that served as the entrance to the room. Again, everyone gasped oohs and ahhs as she nonchalantly pointed to the giant marble pond in the middle of the room.

"That was my bathtub. As you all can appreciate, cleanliness is next to godliness. I used this tub a couple of times every day."

Isabella turned to Charlene, smiled, and said, "I would like you and me to take a walk in my garden. Can you break away for a few minutes?"

Charlene nodded and followed Isabella out the door and down the elevator. Dan, Mattie, Alicia, Bethany, and Amy continued their tour and then ended up standing in the glass-covered solarium surrounding the exit into the gardens, where all kinds of spectacular, exotic tropical flowers hung in pots along the walls and in containers elegantly dropping from the ceiling.

Dan looked out through one of the large windows and then turned to the four girls and said, "Take a look out there. If I am not mistaken, Charlene appears to be in tears. Isabella is hugging her. I think we can assume that Isabella has just announced her intentions of turning this whole plantation into a new location for Charlene's mission."

Amy stepped back from the group and said, "I believe Mattie has told all of you that Isabella has asked me to stay here and help her. She says that she believes the Lord sent me here to take the place of her daughter, who died a few years ago. I know you three are going to be going back home at the end of the summer. I'm going to dedicate the rest of my life to this place."

"The Lord is good,
A stronghold in the day of trouble;
and he knoweth them that trust in Him."
(Nahum 1:7)

Read
More about the
Branson Family

DAN BRANSON NOVEL
No. I

THE LIGHT

- Synopsis -

Dan Branson, an Air Force veteran of the Gulf war, is attracted by a bright light flashing from a location high in Oregon's Cascade Mountains.

He makes the decision to ride into the mountains and search out the source of the flashing light. He is startled when a beautiful woman claiming to have come from "up above" tells him of her mission to provide the Earth's scientists with knowledge of long-forgotten laws of physics.

He mistakenly believes the woman, who calls herself, "Angie," to be an extraterrestrial. Having become a Christian at a young age, he is defensive of her presence and her claims.

Reluctantly, he listens intently as she seeks his support and participation to assist her in her quest. She states that she intends to provide mankind with the tools to save the planet from self-destruction.

Dan, also convinced that society is on a self destruct course, shares his spiritual beliefs as well as his philosophy. He is wary of her but believes in the mission. He recalls his commitment to the Lord and his mission to serve mankind. Ultimately, he accepts the challenge to join her.

Dan experiences opposing forces and unexpected challenges, including several attempts to eliminate him and thwart his efforts to complete the mission.

Angie eventually reveals herself as Angelo, one of God's angels, who had taken on the form of a woman. The challenging story, filled with humor, danger and intrigue, compels the reader to follow the exiting saga to its dramatic conclusion.

Praises for THE LIGHT

Ben Rolphe's *The Light* is spiritually moving and riveting, exploring the concepts of angels, forgotten teachings, and doing God's work on Earth against the backdrop of the rugged wilderness of Oregon's Cascade Mountains. It is one part Western adventure, one part spiritual reminder, one part thriller, and wholly entertaining and riveting.   – Amazon.com

This book tested my beliefs. I am not much of a religious person, but it was a refreshing read with part sci-fi and part theology. I guess it depends on how you view the world and your own spirituality. The character of Dan is well developed, and his story is well written. It was in the outdoors, camping, fishing, and horses. I love them all. And in the end, Dan finds peace with a woman and her daughter.

- Kristine B.

In his latest book, *The Light* Ben Rolphe has used his many talents to give us all a reminder that good things still happen in spite of the terrible times we all face today. In spite of his apparent faith in God and his love for his fellow man, Rolphe is relentless in describing the lack of a belief in God and despair as two of the reasons why men constantly go to war and distrust each other.   – Carolyn F. Piner

This book has its storyline mixed with religion, Christianity, Bible verses, references to angels and demons. It gives you a good storyline and a good ending with a surprise. It really gets your attention, and I found it enjoyable. You learn on many things about the west, life, religion, people and miracles. Everything is fated and people can experience miracles is what the story lets you feel. A good weekend or vacation read.   - Amazon.com

THE LIGHT

(Excerpt)

"Dan, I am going to talk to you now about a subject that will probably sound pretty farfetched but is the reason that I am here and also the reason we selected only *you* to come up here," Angie said as she moved from the log and began to walk slowly around the fire.

She appeared to be in deep thought and was about to answer some of the questions that had been bugging him since she arrived on the scene.

Angie began to talk slowly and with great emphasis that immediately gave him the impression that this was going to be a very heavy conversation.

"We," she hesitated with that statement as she pointed up into the sky, "are convinced that your planet and all of its inhabitants are close to total destruction. Consistent with your opinion and the statements you just made, I believe you have an understanding of what I mean."

Angie walked back over to the log, slid down and sat on the ground just a few feet from Dan. She turned halfway and sat facing Dan. She looked him directly in the eye and said, "This is really serious stuff. To begin with, I am going to inform you as to how little you and your planet know about the galaxy around you. We know that you believe you have identified eight of what you call planets. As a matter of fact, many more of them are up there. Dan, over 400,000 stars and planets exist that your people have yet to discover."

Angie was staring intently at Dan, watching him absorb each word as she continued talking.

"Additionally for some unknown reason, your people have expressed the belief that whatever life exists outside of your world has different forms. Your initial statement to me pertaining to my appearance was that perhaps I had taken some form to resemble you or your people and in fact, I could be a giant lizard. That was really bizarre."

When she mentioned the lizard form, she again let out a chuckle. "You know what, Cowboy? Where I come from, we all look pretty much like, or should I say, *similar* in most respects to the inhabitants of your Earth." She said with a smile.

"I will concede that we have developed the ability to alter our looks or perhaps even take on the appearance of someone else, male or female, in order to fulfill a mission. However, we aren't really much different in our normal form than you," she said.

"Multitudes of living beings are in the galaxy that are much further advanced in technology, however, than the people of Earth. Nearly all of the inhabitants in that galaxy have mastered the ability to live in peaceful coexistence with each other. They know that virtually all of the other inhabitants of the universe, like themselves, have the ability to totally destroy each other," she added.

"Look, Angie, I am having a hard time with all of this, and I think I am going to have to ask you a few questions before you unload more of this doomsday stuff on me," Dan said as he rose and began to walk around the fire pit.

"How did you get here? Where is your spaceship?" he asked with a challenging look on his face.

"Actually, the term 'spaceship' is one you and your society have come up with. That is not to say that countless inter-galactic crafts aren't visiting your planet. Plenty of evidence is present that extraterrestrials have previously visited the Planet Earth. To be more specific, I came here in what we refer to as ninety-one eleven, which has been part of my mission many times in the past. In no time at all, I got here and had even less time to get ready for you," Angie said in a confident tone.

"Okay, so where is this spaceship? Did it just drop you off or have you got it hidden somewhere out of sight? You say ninety-one eleven. To me that sounds pretty close to nine eleven, a date none of Earth's people will ever forget," he said.

"Dan, the spaceship as you choose to call it, actually our 'ninety-one eleven,' is very close. You can't recognize its presence, but it is there. I need to get back to the subject I started with," Angie said, interrupting Dan's train of thought about spaceships.

"I said that we," again she pointed up, "are convinced that the Planet Earth is on a self-destructive course. I am here to see if I may have any influence and what we have to offer your people might change your world and cause you to save yourselves."

"You said what you have to offer? Tell me what you have that we need?"

"That comes later. I need to tell you why we believe that you are close to destroying yourselves from within. We watch your television shows and monitor most of your advertising. Your entire planet is wrestling with more crime and violence than has been witnessed for many centuries. Now you have terrorists who can individually destroy an entire city. Many of them are suicidal and claim they are doing it for religious reasons."

Angie stopped speaking for a moment, got up from her seat on the ground and chose to once again take a seat on the log.

"Tragically, many of the world's youth and a substantial portion of the adults are constantly trying to avoid the reality of life with the excessive use of alcohol and drugs. Your own statistics prove that 50 percent of your marriages and relationships fail. Your society is obsessed with sex. Your merchants can't sell their products unless they use sexual innuendos or scantily-clad females to promote their products or services." Angie stopped speaking and took a deep breath. Her eyes were fixed on Dan, watching for his reaction to her condemning statements.

Finally she began to speak again, this time with a softer tone. "We know about your wife's death and the simultaneous death of your unborn daughter. We also know of the pain that you carry in your heart. The two of you had the kind of love and affection that is needed to perpetuate any society. A large portion of your populous has lost sight of the values that the Creator attempted to instill into people's hearts."

Dan stiffened, fixed his eyes on Angie's and said. "You know about Abby? She was going to have a baby girl? You refer to the Creator. Do you believe in our God? Do you know about our religions?"

Angie was quick to answer. She replied, "Yes, we know all about you and Abby and your unborn daughter. Additionally, there is but one Creator of the entire universe."

THE LIGHT

"This is confusing for us to see that although nearly all of you believe in the existence of the Creator, you all manage to disagree on what the Creator's plans are for all of Earth's people," she said with a sigh.

Dan was quick to confront her statement. "We have a Bible that spells out *exactly* what our God had planned from the very beginning of life. The Holy Bible is an historic account of the Creator, our God, from the beginning of time."

"The fact is that a great deal of division and confusion between the different denominations and belief systems abounds. As I said, we have our Bible, the inspired word of our God. However, not everyone interprets His word in the same way."

"Dan, you were personally participating in a war against the Muslim believers. The Muslim people believe that they are in a Holy War with your people. Do you understand their beliefs? Why do so many people on Earth hate? Dan, if you look into the teachings of the Bible…

Enjoy the rest of this story
by picking up a copy of
The Light today!

CHALLENGED

- Synopsis -

God's messenger, Angelo, asks Dan to fly to South America to assist a Christian cattle rancher. The Mandera family is fourth-generation owners of 20,000 acres of grazing land located in central Argentina. Their son, Don Diego, is not a Christian and has formed an alliance with an international cartel.

The cartel has used threats, murder and violence in their attempts to seize the ranch. The cartel's ruthless actions have taken the lives of two of the ranch's gauchos, as well as critically wounding the ranch's owner, Armando Mandera.

When the ranch's head wrangler was ambushed and killed by the cartel, the Manderas became desperate to locate a Christian leader to bring their herd in from their summer range.

Answering the Lord's call, Dan flies to Argentina to assist the Manderas. The cartel spares nothing in their efforts to stop Dan from helping them.

Upon his arrival in Buenos Aires, he is immediately confronted with attempts to compromise his Christian testimony. Additionally, his flight to the Mandera ranch in a small Cessna aircraft becomes challenging when the pilot, wearing a parachute, jumps from the aircraft.

The intriguing story and the completion of Dan's mission are supported by the intervention and assistance of more than one of God's messengers.

Praises for CHALLENGED

Rolphe penned a very relaxing read—to a Christian, affirming and refreshing; and to a seeker, something to imagine. *Challenged*, the story of Dan and Jessie is well-paced and weaves an enjoyable portrait of family life and a walk with God against the beautiful panorama of nature. If you wonder about God's use of Angels in our lives, this story paints an exciting picture. Could make for a great Christmas gift!   - Karen, Dallas Texas

This is the second Ben Rolphe book I have read, and I enjoyed it as much as I did the first one. Giving his western theme and his religious theme a third element, he takes us off to Argentina where his Angel, Michael, tells him he is needed...and is he ever. He finds himself embroiled in a drug cartel fight.

At home, the ranch is gearing up for a round-up and his daughter wants to go. In fact, the whole family wants to go, but they want him there with them. Trying to solve his problems in Argentina, he may not make it. This is the kind of time when Rolphe's strength in tying everything together is at its best.

The way Rolphe pulls his themes together and makes them interesting is what I look forward to in his books. I look forward mostly to the next one coming out and my having a chance to read and comment on it.

Carolyn F. Piner

Wow! Prior to reading this book, I found out the religious viewpoint of this book. I wasn't sure if it was going to be strictly religious, but I was absolutely blown away by the amazing thriller of a Christian man facing so much serious drama. The author does a terrific job incorporating spirituality and physical situations! Kudos!   - J Croichy

CHALLENGED

(EXCERPT)

Dan was in his office down the hall from the living room when Jessie walked in and sat in one of the leather chairs facing his desk. She sat looking at Dan for a minute while he continued to work on his calculator, obviously deeply engrossed in whatever he was doing.

Finally, she leaned forward and placed a letter with a foreign stamp on it, directly in front of him. Looking up, he reached forward, picked up the envelope and examined both sides before opening it. The handwriting was unfamiliar and the writer had been shaking when the letter was written.

Dear Mr. Branson,

A gentleman who said that he was your friend gave me your name and address. He told me to write to you and explain the problems we are having on our cattle ranch, located here in Central Argentina.

The man's name is Angelo. I am not sure where he comes from, but he just showed up at our ranch a few days ago. I was going to send him on his way, but somehow I felt I should talk to him. Now I believe that he was sent to me by our Lord.

These are very troubled times for my husband and me. I told this man, who calls himself Angelo, about our troubles. He said that he knew someone who could help us with our problems. That is why I am writing to you.

We own a small spread, 8,000 hectares of deeded, grazing land. I am told that in your country, that represents about 20,000 acres. We currently are running about six hundred Hereford cows and their calves. Angelo said that your operation is very similar in size to ours. He also said that he believed you to be the best cattle rancher he had ever met. More important, he told us that you are a dedicated Christian and that you always put your service to our Lord ahead of all else.

Our future and our very lives are currently in jeopardy. Our neighbor is one of the larger South American cartel-owned ranches in the area. I am told that they own and manage 270,000 hectares. They are very wicked people. We are sure that they are being led by Satan. They want our land. They tried to buy our ranch, but we refused to sell. This is our home, and we love it here. Now, they want us to go bankrupt so that they can take over our ranch.

So far these people have shot and killed our head vaquero and one other young man. Two weeks ago, my husband was shot and severely wounded in the leg. He is bed-ridden, and the doctor said he would have to remain immobile for at least another month. After that, he will be restricted to our home and will not be able to ride.

The authorities do not respond to our pleas for help. They are refusing to investigate any of the attacks. We believe that the head of the Policía Federales is being paid to ignore the murders and the attack on Carlos, my husband.

Our vaqueros do not have a leader, and they are all afraid for their lives. We only hire men who have a Christian testimony. We need to begin our round up early in May. However, we are not sure how our vaqueros will respond if they do not have an experienced leader.

Mr. Branson, we are desperate. Angelo told us that you are a very strong man and that he also believes you to have a 'guardian angel' that watches over you and your family. Can you help us? He said that I should tell you that if you see the 'light,' you might want to help us. I don't know what that means, but he said you would.

I should tell you that we are very remote. Our ranch is located in the La Pampa Province of Central Argentina. We are about 400 kilometers from Buenos Aires and 30 kilometers from our nearest city, General Pico.

I pray you can be of help to us.

Very Sincerely,

Teresa Mandera

Dan read through the letter twice before handing it to Jessie. Jessie had been sitting patiently, waiting for him to finish reading. She knew that something of a profound nature was included in the letter as she could see the frowns and deep expressions of concern as he read it.

Jessie also read the letter twice before laying it down on the desk. Now, she looked at Dan who seemed to be mesmerized by the chandelier hanging from the ceiling.

"Are you going to have to go to Argentina?" Jessie asked, looking into Dan's eyes.

Dan changed positions in his leather chair and leaned forward towards Jessie. He looked at the perplexed expression she wore.

"Sweetheart, I don't see how I can ignore this letter. You and I both know that our mutual friend, Angelo, would not have sent her to me unless he believed the Lord wanted me involved. The timing is not good for them or for us. They will be completing their round up, very close to the time that we will be preparing to move our stock onto the upper range."

The two sat silently, looking at each other for what seemed like a long time before Jessie finally spoke. She leaned forward, putting both elbows on the desktop.

"Dan Branson, I don't want you to go to a place like they are describing. It really sounds scary, but I know that if you believe that the Lord wants you to go, you'll have to go. When do you think you'll need to leave?"

"I have to tell you that I am pretty nervous about this whole thing, too. If they are going to do their round up the first week in May, then I have things to do in order to be prepared."

"I will need to write to her and find out how I would get to their ranch. I sure wish I could take Sam with me, but I know that isn't possible. I don't have any idea what quality of horses they have at their ranch," Dan said as he walked around his desk to Jessie.

Jessie stood up from her chair and put her arms around his neck and said, "We talked about this way back when we got married. God's plan brought us together, and we put *His* plan first in our lives. The kids and I will do just fine. I figure you won't be gone more than a month. Am I right? Will you be back in a month or less?" She had a worried look on her face as she looked into Dan's hazel-colored eyes, seeking an answer of reassurance to her question.

"I am going to do everything I can to get back to you and our kids as fast as I can. I am sure that the Lord has everything worked out, and all I have to do is to be prepared to follow His leading. I doubt that this is going to be a piece of cake. These bad guys, whoever they are, have made things pretty rough on these people. I am sure that they will not make things easy for me once they find out that I am throwing in with the Manderas."

Dan moved into the living room and sat down on the comfortable leather couch. He motioned for Jessie to take a seat beside him. They sat for a minute, holding hands, when Dan suggested that they have a word of prayer together.

Dan and Jessie bowed their heads. Dan spoke in a soft voice, "Lord, you are calling me to get involved with these people in Argentina. We need for you to give both of us peace about this calling. I need for you to watch after Jessie and the kids while I am gone. Lord, I also need for you to grant me wisdom and guidance in dealing with the problems facing the…

Enjoy the rest of this story
by picking up a copy of
Challenged…. today!

ABOUT THE AUTHOR

Ben Rolphe and his wife, Anna, reside in North Idaho. As a retired Christian entrepreneur, he has run 16 of his own diversified and profitable companies. He has taught and lectured on marketing and advertising to businessmen and entrepreneur-hopefuls throughout the nation.

His hobbies include world travel, the restoration of antique automobiles and fly fishing. An avid fly fisherman, he has traveled the globe, visiting six of the seven continents, fishing many of the world's famous lakes, rivers and streams.

As a former rancher, he became an excellent horseman and experienced trail rider. While a gentleman farmer/rancher, he experienced the challenges of farming, along with the risks of ranging cattle.

As an Air Force Pilot, he survived twenty-five combat missions during the Korean War. Following military service, he and his family have flown their own aircraft throughout North America, including the remote and primitive areas of the Northwest and Alaska. During his flying career, he has logged over 10,000 hours at the controls of aircraft, both large and small.

His writings, both autobiographical and fictional, reflect many of the locations and experiences of his life.

Contact the Author

www.benrolphe.com